Agon

MYSTIC PROTECTORS SERIES BOOK 2

BY

KATHI S. BARTON

WCP

World Castle Publishing, LLC
Pensacola, Florida

Copyright © Kathi S. Barton 2014
Print ISBN: 9781629891200
eBook ISBN: 9781629891217
First Edition World Castle Publishing, LLC, July 4, 2014
http://www.worldcastlepublishing.com

Licensing Notes

Cover: Karen Fuller
Editor: Eric Johnston
Editor: Maxine Bringenberg

Prologue

Michael moved down the hall toward the office. He knew that the other protectors hated to be summoned to this particular office, but he didn't mind. He loved going in and conversing with the Creator of all things. Boss, as He wanted everyone to call Him, as it sounded so much friendlier, was a man of men. A kind yet firm man, and one who could change things in a beat of a hummingbird's heartbeat. Michael paused in mid-step.

He was going to change things again. Things were running very smoothly right now, and He'd want to shake things up a bit. Michael tried to think what it could possibly be and looked up when someone laughed.

"I was thinking." Boss nodded at Michael's statement. "Am I going to regret coming here today?"

"Possibly. And I know you were thinking. I heard. You think much too hard for a man who has it all." Michael snorted, a habit he'd been trying to break himself of. "You think I would lie to you?"

"Nay. I think You believe whatever You wish will be wonderfully simple when it seldom is."

Boss moved back into the room He'd come from, and Michael followed. The walls were covered with images of the protectors. Protectors had long since been the ones who helped Boss in His daily work. A chosen man or woman would be given the assignment to watch over a child when they took their first breath. They never interfered with the person, but whispered advice, gave them guidance, and when the time was right, they would be there with them when they drew in their last breath as well.

"I do wish to change things. But not for all of my protectors—just a few." Michael sat down, knowing that he'd have to carry out these duties no matter what they were. "You have noticed that they are...unhappy?"

"I have. But it's happened before. They are bored. The last time this happened we gave them a few days to interact on earth and they were happier for it." Boss shook His head. "You do not want that again."

"They wish to leave Me."

Michael sat there, stunned. He'd not heard that. But he knew to leave there would mean—

"I don't want that to happen."

"No, nor do I. Who is it? Maybe I can talk to them." Boss shook His head again. "You don't mean to kill them, do You? I know that is the way of things. When a servant is ready to end their time as a protector, they are sentenced to...please tell me of Your plan."

"I wish to have them...perhaps it would be best if I showed you what I have in mind." The wall took another shape and images, a great many of them, started to move. And the faster they moved, the more movie-like they became. Twice Michael asked Him to slow down, and after He explained it to him, the image moved on. Michael sat there for a long while after the movie stopped, and stared at the images of the few men he'd seen there.

"They will not be happy." Michael looked at Boss but did not reply to His statement. "None of them will."

"Nor will Tholan." Boss smiled as Michael continued. "He will believe that he is not worthy of such a gift."

"He will be the hardest to convince, yes, but if we deal with him later, then perhaps he will see it is not such a bad thing to have happen to him." Michael doubted that. Tholan had a weight on his heart that no one seemed able to help him with. "I would like to start with these five men before Tholan. I want...do you think you could help Me get this started?"

"When would you like for this to happen?" Michael was looking over the files when he realized he'd not been answered. "You have already started this, haven't you?"

"I thought it best that we do some arranging to make sure that the other half of my project was well within hand for us." Boss laughed. "Do not look so crestfallen, Michael. The new group, my Mystics, will be a greater force than we ever imagined."

They worked well into the night, and when Michael left His office, Boss was smiling. Michael would be, too, if he wasn't so worried about Tholan. The man.... Well, that would be something they'd deal with at a later time. But now he had to give the list of men to him and hope that he didn't ask too many questions.

"It is going to be a long time before we will be able to say this worked." Michael heard Boss laugh and flushed. "You should come with me. He will have a fit."

"Nay, he will not. He is a good man, but a man who feels he has failed many. You'll do fine." Boss laughed again. "You are the Archangel, Michael. Men tremble at the sound of your name."

Chapter 1

Judith Craft watched the men walking around the room. She could help them. Hell, it was why she'd been summoned. But they ignored her presence as much as they did the dead man on the floor. She looked at him again and saw things that the others never would.

He'd been killed fourteen hours, eleven minutes, and almost forty seconds ago. And his body, long since cold, held few clues that the officers in the room would be able to detect. But she could see them. It was what she was best at.

There were several hairs on his head that didn't belong to him...two were from the female that had helped kill him, and one was from the man who had found his body. He'd had nothing to do with this man's death, but he did rob him as he waited for the police. The rest of the hairs were from the male who had helped with his demise. She looked down from his head to the wound — the fatal one, as it turned out — that had once been his throat. It had been sliced open with a piano wire.

There was DNA on his shoulders that would not help them in any way. The cops had a large database of information, but these people were not in their system as yet. And even if they were, the dead man had been touched so many times by others in the room that it would be corrupted and not of any use to them. But it was to her.

The buttons on his shirt also held information. This she could use in ways that the cops never would. It held data that Judith could use to not just capture the woman, but find her as well. She watched as a man from the hospital leaned down to look at something and sneezed on the body. Well, she would have been able to find her. Now all she would be able to find was the man now blowing his nose, too. Judith looked up when the man who had called her stepped in front of her.

"They are ready for you...no, that's not right. They're going to let you see him now, but they don't think you can help." She nodded and followed him to the dead man. "Just so you know, I think what you can do is amazing, but there are others that—"

"They think I'm a kook." Benny turned to look at her and smiled. "I really don't care. You either want me to help you or you don't. It matters little to me."

"I know that." She moved to the body and noticed something she'd missed before. "The man was dying. Did you know that?"

"We don't have a name as yet. His wallet and all his personal belongings are gone but for the clothes on his body. There aren't even imprints here that anyone can find. It's as if he'd been brought here, killed, and left."

"He was." Judith touched the small button and shook her head. She'd been right. There was nothing for her to feel. When she moved to the other side of the body, she spoke to Benny. He was the only man, the only cop, she'd ever trusted, and there were days she wasn't so sure about that either.

"His name is Oscar Grand. He worked for a printing company not far from here. I think he was on his lunch break or something that had him at a restaurant when he was taken." She took the gloves when Benny handed them to her, but didn't put them on. She had no idea what he thought she'd feel from the body if she couldn't touch it, but continued. "There are hair strands on the left side of his head just over his ear. They belong to the female that was here when the male arrived with Grand. She was here waiting for them."

"Two people killed him?" She nodded and watched as he plucked the hairs from where she pointed on Oscar's head. "I don't suppose you know who they are, do you?"

"Not yet." He just nodded and she glanced up at him as she continued. "The female is new to this, but the male isn't. He's less hesitant than she is. That's why you'll find some of the stab wounds more sure than the others. He's done this before. He is also the one who garroted him. It's his...signature, I guess you'd call it."

"Do you know if he's done this in this state?"

Judith shrugged. She could have told him that they would find two more bodies soon, both of them killed by the same man, but she didn't. She was there for this murder and not the others. Not yet at any rate. Judith could also have told Benny how he'd done it, but didn't.

"Are they local?"

She looked up at him with a grin. "I'm good, but not that good. He wasn't killed here like you said, but he did finally die here. They intended for him to die much slower, but the man pulled too tightly on the wire and he was dead before they could get whatever they wanted from him. They wanted the combination to the safe where he works. Apparently he owed the woman something."

"Do I even want to know?"

She shrugged again. What did she care if the woman had let the man fuck her for a freebie and had come to collect?

"What can you tell me about the male? Is he old, young? Maybe even a little bit, like if you know his name?"

"I don't know any of that, but he's killed before but not fingered by you guys. Also, the female is an unknown as yet for you. But you'll see more of her in the coming weeks if you don't catch her—"

"What the fuck is she doing here?"

Judith didn't turn to look at the man who had come into the room bellowing as if no one in the room could hear him. Benny stood to stand behind her, to protect her she supposed, but she didn't need him to. Judith had been caring for herself longer than anyone else had.

"She was called in to identify the body." Sort of true, but she didn't correct Benny when he spoke to the other man. Denis Pallor hated her with a passion and would steamroll anyone that tried to gainsay him. And Benny was forever pissing the commissioner off.

"I guess she just happened to be in the neighborhood again." Judith stood and turned to look at the man. He took several steps back from her and she smiled. Her height made men uncomfortable, and she loved rubbing it in this man's face that she was a great deal taller than him.

"Commissioner? How's it hanging?"

He sputtered for a few seconds before he turned back to Benny. She decided it was time for her to go. Benny would come by later if he needed anything else from her. That was the way they worked.

Judith was home nearly an hour when she heard someone knocking on her door. She looked at the monitor on her counter and smiled at the woman standing there. Lily Anderson was Benny's wife, and when he was being watched, she'd come to get whatever it was Judith had found out. Judith moved through her small apartment to the front of her shop door and thought of the years she'd known these two.

Had it not been for Benny she might well have been as dead as the man she'd just helped him with. But he'd seen something in her abilities that no one else had seen. He'd given her a means to use them for something other than causing pain, and she'd been at his beck and call since. Lily smiled at her when she opened the door.

"He's in a meeting and sent me to pick up some tea for him." Judith handed her a file and a thermos of hot tea. "I had a favor to ask you as well. I was wondering if you'd come to a friend of mine's house and identify a few plants. She is trying to fix the herb garden that came with the house, and we can't find some of the plants in a book we got. It's an old garden, but it's in poor shape."

"Sure." Judith sat down behind the counter after pulling a few of her favorite books out from under it. When Lily sat down as well and leaned back on her couch, Judith pulled out her freshest jam and some scones she'd made the day before. The hot tea was sitting on the small oak table she'd picked up at an auction a few days ago. "I would like to have a few cuttings if they're something I don't have. Is that okay?"

"I told her you might and she said it would be fine. You'll like her. Her name is Kala Trainer. She and her husband bought the Carpenter house." Judith knew the place but had never been there. Lily told her that it was being renovated now. "They should have most of the bedrooms done in a few days, and the furniture has been in storage. I thought we could go out today. Now if you're not busy."

Judith didn't answer her but got up to get a couple more books that she was going to take with her. Her intentions were to veg out in front of the television that night, but Benny had called and she'd changed her mind, along with what she was having for dinner. The steak no longer appealed to her.

"Does she...have you spoken to her about me? I mean, I don't care for people. You know that." Lily took two of the scones, and Judith ate three before she continued. "Can't you just bring me a cutting and I'll tell you what I think they are?"

"I could, but I'd rather you came out to the house with me. It's just Kala and I for now. The men are working at the other end of the property and won't be back for a long time. I want to make sure that the ones we've marked are what we think they are."

Judith heard the timer in the kitchen and nearly let the thing go, but knew that she'd have a mess in her kitchen if she did. Having very little choice, she got up to see to the pots she had there. Lily, of course, followed.

"I don't want to leave here." Lily sat at the counter while Judith poured the hot mixture into little jars. When she was putting the lids on the fresh jams, she realized that Lily hadn't said anything. She looked at Lily with a raised brow.

"You're finished then?" Judith nodded before she could think that she shouldn't. "My car is out front. We should hurry so that we can get you back here before you turn into a pumpkin."

It was an old joke between them…at least it was a joke to Lily and Benny. They both would bully her into things she would never do on her own. It mattered little to either of them that she didn't want to do whatever it was, so long as she did what they wanted. Today wasn't going to be any different.

Grabbing her jacket, she locked up her house and shop and moved out the door, setting the alarms as she left. She wasn't going to take a chance on anyone coming in except the people who knew just how to get in. And they were very few. Turning, she looked at Lily as she stood on the sidewalk, and Judith had an overwhelming urge to touch her hand.

Instead of acting on what would no doubt be horrific, Judith shoved her hands into her pockets and got into the car. She never touched until she had to.

~~~

Kala wrote as fast as she could but knew she was missing things. Looking over at Alison, her cook, she wondered why she wasn't making notes. Of course, the woman could cook anything without looking at a recipe a thousand times, and was more than likely remembering every little detail. Kala looked at the woman who had gotten out of the car only an hour ago.

To say she was pretty would have been an understatement. She was more than that. Her looks—porcelain skin, dark hair and eyes—made Kala think of exotic dancers she'd seen on television once. The kind that did things with their hips that she had always envied. Kala realized that she was speaking to her when Lily nudged her from behind.

"You do go off into your own world, don't you?" Kala smiled rather than get angry. Valyn told her the same thing when he caught her thinking hard. "I asked if you were okay with me taking some of these pieces with me."

"Of course." Judith knelt down and started digging at the root of the pink delphinium that had been deemed a weed until Judith had told them what it was. She said that she could use the pink color for things. "What is it you do with this stuff? If you tell me you make the most scrumptious cookies with them, I might kidnap you to bake for me."

Her slight pause had Kala looking at Lily. There was something there, but she wasn't sure if she wanted to know. When Judith continued digging in the garden at the other herbs she'd identified for her, Kala started to ask again. But Judith spoke first.

"I make jellies and jams. Sometimes soaps and teas, depending on what I have in stock from my own garden. I have a shop in the front of my place that is open most days, but I don't do tricks." Her statement had Kala looking at Lily as Judith set the tiny plants in the crockery pots she'd brought with her and continued. "What did you really want to know, Mrs. Trainer? I mean, Lily said you knew that I helped Benny. Did you want me to answer some age old question for you?"

Her tone led Kala to believe that the woman was pissed off at her and her anger surged forward. "No. If I wanted answers I would ask for them right out. I was simply asking you what you'd need herbs for if, as you said when you got here you didn't cook all that much. There is no reason for you to take that sort of attitude with me. I'm not usually a person who beats around the bush, and I like my information that way as well. Suck it up, Judith, no one here wants you to perform for them like a bear."

Judith stood up and seemed to tower over her for several seconds before she took a step back. When she did, Kala had a feeling she'd passed some test and wanted to ask her what it was. But the look in the other woman's eyes had her staring back at her.

"You're having sons. Four of them." Kala put her hand over her small mound and nodded. "They're...I don't think you're human. Are you?"

"No. I'm not." She had no idea why it seemed important not to lie to this woman, but Kala didn't. "Most of the people here aren't, but I'm sure you already knew that, didn't you?"

"I did." Judith picked up her five little pots and moved toward the car. Kala wanted to ask her what she was but wasn't sure if she really wanted to know. At least not yet, at any rate. The woman wasn't scary or anything like that, but she was....

"Who hurt her?" Lily only shook her head when she asked her. "Someone did. She has no trust whatsoever, does she?"

"No. It took Benny years to get her to trust him. And longer still for me to be able to come to her house and not get tossed out on my bottom. What else have you noticed about her?"

Kala looked at Judith again and tried to think what it was about her that had seemed so wrong when Kala had first seen her. There was something so very...then it hit her. She looked at Lily.

"She has no protector." Lily shook her head and Kala wondered how the hell that had happened and asked.

"I don't know. I asked Boss about it and He just smiled at me. You know how He is. If He wants you to know, He'll tell you, but mostly you have to work it out on your own." Yeah, Kala knew that.

Boss had been to her house a lot in the past few months since she and Riss had married. Mostly it was to argue with her, but sometimes they'd have a good laugh or two. She really enjoyed the man but this wasn't right. She decided to get to the bottom of it as soon as she could.

All in good time. Kala nearly screamed when Boss spoke to her through her mind. She hated when He did that, and He knew it. *I have a plan for every creature. Did you not know that by now? Even you have a greater purpose than being the mother of the first children born of protectors, and even more than being Riss's wife. You are very…curious, are you not?*

She decided to ignore His comment about her plans. *And what of her plans? Who will take care of her when she needs it? Who gives her encouragement when she feels like she is failing?* He didn't answer her as she made her way to the car. Lily told her that she had to get Judith back before it got too much later.

She is…I have tried to give her protectors but she runs them off with her temper. I have never met…she is more stubborn than you are at times. And this child is like that all the time. But I will tell you that I have been watching her, but from afar.

Kala sat on the porch when the car was out of sight, and Boss appeared beside her. He sat down and looked out over the yards before He continued. "Judith has a gift. Not unlike a protector's gift in that they can see each other, but hers is deeper, stronger than some. I have had Benny and Lily watching her for years. I'm sure she is aware of them and why they come to her, but she does help them, too. It is a love-hate relationship, I believe. But she does help them and for now, that is enough."

"Lily said she helped Benny solve murders, but I'm betting it's more than that. He said that she can see things on a body that modern science cannot. And know things about a death that he'd never know without her help." He nodded but said nothing. "Why? Is it a gift as you called it, or did something happen to her to give her this?"

His laughter made her look at Him. Boss always seemed so tired to her, and she wondered if He was resting. Without voicing her question to Him, she knew what He would say. He was getting enough. How much, to the man who watched everyone all the time, was enough? she wondered.

"It was forced upon her by an accident at birth. My fault, if you wish to lay blame." When He said no more, she wondered what might befall her own unborn children. "They will be fine, my dear. As will our girl. I have great plans for her. You'll see."

"Another protector is going to meet his match, I take it." His smile had her wondering which man would find as much happiness as she and Riss had. "I suppose if I asked you'd not tell me."

"I would not. But I am glad that you have not thought it wrong of Me to do this." He leaned back in His seat and grinned. "I will tell you that she will not come into this happily. I'm sure you will agree with Me when I tell you she is a little on the stubborn side."

"A little? I think she might have written the book on it. In the few minutes she was here, I think I might have come to the conclusion she hates me. Not just me but all people. Is that true?" He nodded and it broke Kala's heart to see the sadness bloom on His face. "She doesn't believe in You either, does she? Not even a little."

"No. She does not believe in anything, as a matter of record. Not that I blame her much, because she has good reason not to trust. But she will need to before this is finished." He looked at her. "I've come to ask you for your help with her."

Kala had so much to do now she barely had time to do it all. But she'd do anything for Boss even if she had to let things go. She thought of the woman again and told Him she'd help Him.

"But I'd like to know what it is she can do, or as much as you can tell me about her, please. I know what I've been told, but I have a feeling there's more to it than that." He nodded but didn't say anything. "Okay, I can see you're going to be a pain in the ass about this. At least tell me why she hates people so much. If you want my help, I need yours too."

"When she was but a child, smaller than the ones you carry now, a man harmed her mother. She was left in a state that rendered her brain no longer functioning. Her father, a man of less faith than the daughter, had her mother held in a state of flux until the babe could survive outside of the womb. He was going to raise the child on his own and keep her safe." Kala wanted to tell him she no longer wanted to know, but he continued. "After a time, the man knew that his child, Judith, was not like other children. She could do things with her mind that he knew would cause him embarrassment if anyone could see it. Moving pencils and bending objects at first. Then she could see things that no others could. Things that had not yet happened, as well as things people had tried to hide from others. Her father, he took to...hurting young Judith whenever her deformity, as he called it, would show."

"What sort of things can she do?" He looked at her and Kala pleaded, "Please tell me. I need to know so that I can help her."

"Her mind can process things faster than a computer. She can read a thick book in minutes, add equations that would boggle even the most learned man, and she can see things, small details that other would not." She asked Him if that was all, and He shook His head as He finished. "With a simple thought she can move mountains."

Kala waited for Him to tell her He was exaggerating, but He looked out over the field again. She listened as He told her the rest of her story. It was one she was sure would haunt her for months, if not years.

"He was not a man who should have been given such a gift. I knew that then. But that is what I had at the time and it was too late when it came to pass for me to change it. The child he had would have loved him above all things, yet he destroyed that with his fists and words. There were times when she would try so hard to please him, doing anything he asked of her, until he tried to have her cheat for him. She would not give him the information he so wanted, and he nearly destroyed her for it." He looked at her as He continued. "She needs only to touch someone or something to have it tell her everything about it. Where it has been, who the person has touched, as well as who might have killed him. Her father wanted her to touch the dealers on their street so he could find where deals were going to happen. His plan was to take the money after the deal by killing the dealer when it was most convenient for him. Then use it for...well, purposes that Judith found to be distasteful."

If Judith could tell what the future might hold for someone she touched, then the possibilities were endless in what she could know. "Could she even tell who her father had murdered? Where the bodies were when he did it? She could...he wanted her to tell him things that he'd gain from. Like lotto numbers and such." He nodded and turned back to the field. "She could have made him wealthy beyond any dreams he had, I'm thinking, and she wouldn't help him because it was wrong. Can she tell...did she know that he'd die too?"

"She did. But it did him little good when it came to it. The man...his own brother, sadly...killed him right in front of our girl. Murdered him, and she believes it was her fault. So at the age of thirteen she was alone, but had by that point gotten better at hiding what she did not want the others to know about her. The uncle knew, of course, and now...well, now he has it in his mind that she will help him. Now out of prison and looking for the child, she will be in grave danger."

"He wants to use her. Use her just like her father wanted. But she won't, will she? She'll continue to say no until...he'll kill her, won't he?" Boss nodded, and Kala tried to think of all the things a terrible man could and would use Judith's talents for. It was depressing as well as overwhelming.

Kala sat there a long time after Boss left her. All she could think about was how horribly Judith had been treated, and how the one person who should have been there for her had failed her the worst of all. She knew how the girl felt on that level. Kala looked up when a shadow fell over her. Riss sat beside her.

"I have spoken to Boss. He said that He felt you were upset when He left you. I think He was very worried and sent me to you." She nodded and pulled his hand to cover their babies. "He is active today, is He not?"

Kala smiled. She wanted to tell Riss that they were having four boys, not just the one, but she wanted him to be surprised. It was getting harder and harder for her to hold onto the secret with each week that went by. But when their child moved under her skin, she knew that they were the luckiest people in the world. Laying her head on his shoulder, she decided that she wanted everyone in the world to be as happy as she was at that very moment.

"I want to go into town tomorrow. I have someone I'd like to meet on her grounds. I think...she might be able to help Lily and me with our projects." Riss grinned and she could see the devilment in his eyes. "What do you know?"

"That Judith will become a part of our family, and even though I know not who he is, I know he will be happy soon, too." Kala hoped so, but she had a feeling whoever he was, he might be more upset than anything. None of the protectors she knew were all that keen on becoming wedded.

Chapter 2

"You want me to watch this person from afar but to only intervene when she is in mortal danger. I do not understand this." Agon waited for Tholan to explain, but all he did was sit there staring at him. "Where is her protector now? Shouldn't he be here telling me what he knows about her?"

"From what I have been told, she has none." Agon wasn't sure he'd heard him right so he asked him to repeat it. "I said she has none, and when she does have one, she is...let us just say that she has none. There was someone who watched over her for a while, but something happened. And before you bully me into telling you what it was, I do not know. I have been told she has fallen through the walls."

"Walls?" It took Agon a second to understand. "You mean cracks? She has fallen through the cracks and no one noticed before today?" Tholan nodded and Agon felt himself grow madder.

"It will not be long, Agon, just a few...she will only need you to watch her for a little while. I'm to understand that she will have someone permanent in a few days. A week at the most." Agon was shaking his head. "I know that you are in need of your time off, Agon, but I have no one else. They are all working around the clock as it is."

"I'm exhausted." He was, too. His charge had died two days ago from a horrific accident. He'd only been thirty-two years old. "I'm not...I don't know if I can do this right now. I really enjoyed that man and was...he left behind five children and a wife." And a hole in Agon's heart, though he didn't mention that. He knew that each of them lost a part of their heart when their charge died like this.

"I know. I'm terribly sorry. But this woman, you will not have to get close to her. In fact, I was warned that the more distance you put between the two of you the better. She can see us." Agon felt his body turn to ice. To see them was something no one was supposed to be able to do. Before Agon could ask him, Tholan raised his hand. "I know nothing save she can see us and does not like to have anyone near her. I have...there was another protector as of yesterday, but he came to me and said he would quit now if he had to stay with her a moment longer. He told me she was not nice. I could not get him to tell me how she had mistreated him; he would only say that she is not nice."

"Most humans now are not nice sometimes, but that is no reason for him to leave her unattended." Agon started to pace back and forth when the door to Tholan's office burst open. Michael stood there with his sword drawn and a look of fear on his face. Agon reached for his own weapon before remembering that he'd given his up decades ago.

"You will come with me now."

Agon took a step toward Michael only to be brought up short. The room they were now in was not Tholan's office, and the amount of blood all over the place had him wishing he'd taken the time to arm himself. He saw the woman seconds before she looked right at him.

"Before you go all medieval on me, I didn't kill him. When I got here, he was already dead. The police have been called, and Benny is on his way." Agon looked behind him and realized she was speaking to him. "I think someone broke into my shop while I was gone. David here was picking up his order, but he had the code to get in. He's been coming and going here for years and had never had a problem. And now this. As I said, I've called the police already."

"David is the man there?" She nodded and took a step back when he moved toward her. "I am only going to see if you are wounded as well. My name is Agon, in the event you wish to know."

"I don't, but whatever. And I'm not hurt, you moron. I just told you he was here when I got here. What the hell are you doing here anyway?" Agon looked for Michael to have him explain because, to be honest, he had no idea where here was. "What's the matter with you? Who are you looking for? I asked you a question. What are you doing here?"

"I do not know, to be perfectly honest." Agon noticed that not only was Michael not with him, but he was reasonably sure that this was the woman he was supposed to care for over the next week. "What's your name?"

"As if I would share that information with a total stranger." She looked at the phone, then back at him. "Did that other man...I don't remember his name, the idiot from the other day...did he send you? The other protector? I swear to you that you guys get dumber daily."

"I do not have a clue who you might mean." He had a feeling she meant the protector who refused to watch her, and just knew that Michael had set him up. "I have been assigned to watch over you until someone permanent can come in and keep an eye on you. Can you tell me your name?"

"No, I will not. You're supposed to know that, aren't you? And that's supposed to make me feel better how, that you're coming to protect me without a clue as to who I am?" He shrugged and watched her for any sign that she'd try to harm herself. "I don't want you here. In fact, I think you should go back to wherever you came from and tell them if they send another person here with plans of watching me, I might buy a gun and shoot the lot of you."

"It will do you little good. We are immortal." He had no idea why he found her to be funny, but he did. And he wanted to bait her more. Her anger showed on her face like a shield, and he wanted to see it crumble. "You could shoot me, I suppose, but it would do you little good. It may, more than likely, go through me and into the wall, but it will not kill me. There will be pain, of course. What sort of gun were you hoping to purchase? In my life, I have seen many guns that—"

"Stop."

He'd been moving toward her and found the fact that she'd noticed his movements funny as well. Laughing heartily, he moved another step toward her, only to be brought up short when she pulled out a gun. He'd been telling the truth when he told her she couldn't kill him, but it would hurt.

"I'm not shitting you. Stay the hell away from me. I've told that other guy several hundred times I wish to be left alone."

"Are you afraid of me?" Agon watched her face and saw that while she was angry, it wasn't necessarily directed fully at him. "As I am only going to be here for a little while, why do you not tell me your name?"

"You don't have that little file on me? The other guy did. He was always quoting things from it for me as if I hadn't lived it. He was a class-A dumbass." Agon lifted his hands to show her they were empty. "That doesn't mean you don't have it somewhere. I think he is off his noodle a bit. And you are, too, if you think that I don't notice that you're still moving in my direction."

"I should still like to check to make sure that you have not been harmed in some way. As for your other protector, I do not know who he is so I cannot tell you." This time when he moved, it was to be standing within a foot of her. "Can you tell me who hurt your friend?"

He wasn't sure he liked the way his voice sounded. Agon had a deep voice that matched his size, he'd been told. But looking at the woman in front of him, he was both pleased and a little overwhelmed that she could almost look him in the eyes. Agon found he wanted to pull her closer to him until she was flush with his body, but didn't understand why that sounded so appealing to him either.

"I don't know his name yet, but he came here when I expressly told them that I didn't want anyone watching over me. I think he was sent by my...do you think you could back the fuck up?" Agon told her he could but didn't move. "The point is, I don't want you this close. Not here at all, as a matter of fact, but since I know you won't go until I have to hurt you, backing up would be nice."

"You're very tall, are you not?" She didn't move immediately, and when she started to back away from him, he was pleased to see that she had nowhere to go. "Look at me, please?"

"Go away." He lifted her chin up and felt her heat through his fingers. He'd never touched a human before and was surprised at how warm they were. Her breath touched his skin, and he felt as if he could breathe her into him. It was a strange yet appealing feeling, and he wanted to explore more of it.

The urge to kiss her had him lowering his head. Agon, like all protectors, had no experience with the human form and even less with females. But this woman had him thinking things, even wanting to act on them, that he'd never felt before. Just before his lips touched hers, a sound behind him had him shoving her behind him as he spread his wings to protect her.

"Oh." He stared at Kala for some seconds before he realized that he'd shown himself to a human, the woman behind him. When the woman skirted around him, he wanted to reach for her again, but she was out of his reach before he could. Looking at Kala, he felt his face heat with shame. He'd nearly broken a protector law. And to be honest, he wasn't even sure that he cared that he had.

"Christ, it's like Grand Central around here. If you're here about the dead man, save it. This guy is just leaving and so are you, as a matter of fact." Kala looked at the woman when she spoke, then at him. Agon wanted to tell her he was going nowhere, but the look on Kala's face had him pause.

"What has happened? Is it the baby? Have you been harmed by the man who killed this one?" He took a step toward Kala and stopped when the woman stepped in front of her. Agon had never had someone think he'd harm someone before. "You think to protect her from me? I would die for her."

"And you just might if you don't back up. Have you ever had someone say that to you as much as I have? If so, then you might want to read up on people's bubbles. It might help you a great deal." He took a step back, wondering at the violence this woman would resort to just to protect someone she didn't know. But he could see that no matter what, she would try her best to kill him—or anyone, for that matter—if they tried to hurt Kala. He nodded as he took several steps back.

"I will stand here." Kala laughed when the woman huffed at him. Agon had no idea why, but he wanted to pick the young woman up and take her somewhere that was private. He felt his cock harden more, and he stepped behind the table to adjust himself. He'd never felt this…this hard before.

"I came to see if you could help me with a project. But I can see that you're…and are you aware there is a dead man on your floor?" There was humor in Kala's voice, and Agon had a feeling she'd seen more than he'd thought. He wondered if she would tell anyone that he'd been about to kiss the younger woman, but then realized Kala knew her.

"I came back here and I found him…David was supposed to be picking up product. I let him have the lockout code so that I don't…why are you here again?" The woman looked at him. "Why are you still here? I think I've made it abundantly clear that you are not wanted or needed here."

Ignoring her for the moment, he looked at Kala. There was still the smile that gave him chills for some reason, one that told him she knew something that he did not. Agon was not used to people looking at him this way.

"I wish her name, please?" Both women looked at him, and he smiled as charmingly as he could. "It would help me in my duties if I did not have to call you woman all the time."

Kala was nearly brimming with laughter, and Agon smiled more. There was something going on here, and he wanted to know what it was. He liked a good joke and laugh as much as the next person. Before Kala could tell him anything, the woman spoke.

"I don't care what you call me so long as it's not where I can hear you. I think I've asked you like a dozen times to leave here, yet here you still are. Don't you have anything better to do with your time?"

"I do not." He leaned back against the table and crossed his arms over his chest. "I have been assigned to care for you. I take my duties very seriously. The fact that I wish to kiss you is a bonus."

"You most certainly will not be kissing me." He watched as her tongue came out and moved along her lips, wetting them, seemingly, for him. He felt his cock stretch more and wondered about that as well. He'd never in all his life had a reaction like this to anyone. He looked at Kala when she cleared her throat.

"Her name is Judith. Judith Craft. She was out at the house yesterday helping me identify the plants in the herb garden." Agon watched Judith's face and wondered what it was about her that had him wanting to run for his life and take her into his arms at the same time. When something occurred to him, he straightened up suddenly.

"Oh no." They both looked at him as the realization of what was going on started to wash over him. "Oh, I will not let this happen to me. I do not want a female in my life. I will not...I knew that there was something going on when I was asked to come and watch her for a few days. I will not have it. I do not...I shall speak to Boss about this. You will...this is not going to...I will not have a wife."

Kala shook her head and started forward when he backed away from them both. It was Michael. He'd done this to him. And Agon was not going to be trapped as Riss had been. He closed his eyes and willed himself to his room, only to open his eyes and see that he was still with the woman. Before he could try again, a sound from the outside had him leaping to both women and pulling them beneath his opening wings. Gunfire sprayed the front of the house even as he protected them. Agon had no idea what had happened, but there was no way he was leaving her until he had some answers. She was his to protect for the moment, but there would be no marriage between them.

~~~

Riss held Kala to him even as the rest of the protectors helped clean up the mess of the front of the house. He had not been there when she needed him was all he could think about. And his child...their child...had been in harm's way as well.

"We're fine." He nodded but didn't let her go. "Riss, I have to go and see to Judith. She looks like she's going to scream at any moment. I don't think she's very good around crowds of people. The poor girl looks so unsure of herself and I feel sorry for her. And poor Agon; you should go and talk to him."

He could see that as well. Judith's entire body looked strung tight, like at any moment she would snap. The police gave her a wide berth, but they each kept their eyes on her. He started for Agon when Kala pulled away to go to Judith. But Benny cut him off, and he decided to speak to him first.

"I don't know what happened, so don't even ask me. Agon has asked me a dozen times in the few minutes I've been here." Riss looked at his friend, who, while standing close to Judith, seemed to be keeping his distance as well. Neither of them looked all that happy. "She said she doesn't know what's going on either, but I know she's lying. If anyone would know, it would be her. And the guy that was killed in here, he was a friend of hers, and I think she's feeling guilty about that, too."

"Kala said Judith could see things and that she helps you on occasion with your investigations. Is that true?" Benny nodded and looked around the room when he did. "She is terrified, is she not? Not of the bodies strewn about the street and room, but of you as well. Because there are so many of you, correct?"

"I would say that's a good assessment. And she doesn't do well with people on a one-on-one basis, but this is going to make her blow up." Riss nodded and looked at Judith again while Benny continued. "Someone wanted her dead, I would say, or at the very least, for her to come help them, too. And had we not been on our way here anyway, I'm not sure what would have happened. The three dead men outside opened fire on my men the moment they got out of their cruisers. I think they were going in to finish the job, whatever that might have been."

Riss watched Kala speak to Judith, but it was apparent that the woman wanted them all gone. He was going to talk to her as soon as the body was taken away. Agon walked toward him like a man who had been told he was about to do something he did not want to do.

"She will not let me near her. I am not sure I want to be, but I have a need to comfort her." Riss knew the feeling very well. "I think I am also being targeted by Michael. I believe he thinks she is going to be my wife. I was just on my way to speak to him when the men started to fire into this room. She was lucky not to have been injured."

Riss looked at Judith, then back at his friend. If there were two more ill-suited people, he wouldn't want to meet them. Where Agon was outgoing and friendly, Judith was standoffish and, well, not friendly. He decided to see Michael as soon as he could.

Benny was talking to Judith when Riss moved toward her. There was something very cautious about her, and he knew it had little to do with today.

"She was hurt more than you can know." He looked at Michael when he appeared beside him. "Do not speak to me. No one can see me but you. I've come to tell you that Agon is correct and that Judith is what he believes her to be."

Riss moved toward the back door and into the smallish yard behind the house. It was small because of the huge building that occupied nearly all of the space. There were perhaps three feet between the door he'd just come out of and the one that led into the building. He looked at Michael when he appeared before him.

"He is not happy with you. And I would say he will do everything within his power to keep his distance from her." Michael nodded and smiled. "I know it will do him little good, but he might make her more upset before it comes to pass. She will not be happy either, but he will harm her heart if he continues to shove her away and pull her close to him."

"I do believe that Miss Craft can fend for herself, do you not?" Riss nodded and smiled. "She is a little more headstrong than I would have chosen for him, but they will suit as well as you and Kala have. Their relationship will be livelier than yours, but I think no less happy for the match."

"He has told me that he will not take to this. And I do not know how to help him." Michael told him not to. "What if he should come to me? What should I tell him?"

"He will come to you. If I were you, I would advise him to stay away from her and to keep his distance. It worked for you. The more you were told to stay away, the more you wanted the young Kala." Riss flushed when he thought of how many times he'd been warned to stay away from his charge, only to seek her out more and more. He looked at the house again and felt sorry for his friend.

"Agon will be most displeased with us." Michael nodded. "I shall stay out of it, but I would enjoy being made aware of things. It might help me in answering his questions."

"I will tell you what I can." As Michael disappeared, Riss sat on the tiny bench near the building. He wanted to go inside. The smells coming from the open window of the building felt as if they were calling to him. There were so many scents floating around him that he closed his eyes to imagine the beautiful plants that he knew they came from.

"What are you doing here?" He looked at Judith as she stood in front of him. He'd not heard her coming out of the house and stood up. She backed up several steps, and Riss felt badly about scaring her. "I asked you a question."

"I came out to get some fresh air and to speak to a friend of mine." She looked around, and he chuckled. "I'm afraid he has gone back to work. Are things straightened out with the police? I shall have some of the protectors replace the windows that were broken out if we can."

"They're gone, finally. I don't know how straightened out they are, but they left anyway." She looked back at the house. "That man, Agon, can you make him leave me alone? I've tried to explain to him that I don't want him here, but he insists on staying for some stupid reason."

"No, I cannot. I'm sorry, but he is to protect you. And from what I have heard, he did his job well today."

She nodded and turned back to Riss. He saw the fear there and also something else. But before he could figure out what it was, she stiffened. Riss felt his wings stretch from his body. He wasn't sure what it was that had startled her, but he was going to protect what he already considered his family.

"Do you all have those?" He nodded and left them where they were, spread from his body wide and full. He had no idea why he felt so at ease here with her, but he did. "Does he have them as well, and are they this big?"

"Agon? Yes he has wings, though I believe his are bigger than mine. He is a large man." She walked around him but kept her distance, too. He let her, knowing that she wouldn't touch him, and it saddened him for some reason. "His are wider than mine. I have been...when I was created, there was little use for them. Agon was made a decade later, and we found that our wings could be used to protect, not just fly. He can cover a great deal of area with his."

"He said he wants to kiss me." Judith was behind him so he had no idea what was on her face when she said that. "I don't want him near me. Especially not to touch me. I can…I have this freaky way about me, and I can see things when I touch people."

"You are gifted, not freaky." She huffed at him, and Riss smiled. "Benny says that you help him on cases. He said that you have solved a great many cases for him that he would have otherwise left as cold cases."

"His boss hates me. The commissioner says I'm a waste of taxpayer's money. I don't know how he figures that when I've never taken any money from his precious department." Riss turned then, bringing his wings to his body. She was leaning against the building and looking at the dark, wooden fence that surrounded her property. "I don't think he is the one that sent those men for me, but I think he knows about it. If that man Agon stays here, he'll get hurt. I've got enough shit going on right now, and watching some guy who thinks I need protecting isn't on my list of favorite things to do today."

"He cannot die." She nodded and looked at him. Riss felt her pain as if he was sharing it with her. He supposed in a way he was. "Has he harmed you? In any way, has he harmed you?"

"Agon?" Riss nodded. "No, and I won't let him either. I've been…let's just say I've had enough pain in my life and I'm fed up with it. I have to go to work."

The abrupt change of subject startled him, and before he could catch up with her, she was moving into the building. Just as the door closed behind her, the one to the house opened and Agon stepped out. He did not look any happier than the girl had.

"She is in there?" Riss nodded and watched as Agon paced in front of the door. Riss wondered if he was aware that he was talking to himself when Agon suddenly turned to him. "She is my wife. Not my wife as yet, but I think Michael has set me up. And when I've tried to see him, he tells me he is much too busy today."

"And that would be bad for her to be your wife, Agon?" Agon nodded, then shook his head. "I see. You want her, but not enough to be...I think it is called 'saddled' with her. I can think of many things that one would regret being saddled with, but a beautiful woman is not it."

"She is not going to be my wife. In any way, Riss." Riss nodded as Agon started pacing again. "I want to touch her. Feel her body close to mine and kiss her. I have a need to taste her mouth to see if it tastes as good as I think it might. Then there is my body. I cannot control it around her. I run so hot and hard that I feel as if the world knows that I need her in ways that are not right."

"She will taste better than you can ever dream of, and her body will give you pleasure in ways you cannot imagine." Agon stared at him for several seconds. "But you cannot touch her. She is your charge. If you do not wish to have her as your wife, then you must not touch her in any way. If you do...if you do, my friend, then there will be no turning back. For the touch of the woman you are to spend your days with will haunt you in ways that will make you want to end your life in order to be with her. Trust me on this. I am well aware of how your body will crave her, and you will stop at nothing to have her again and again."

"I do not want her." Riss nodded and could see that Agon was lying to him as much as he was himself. "She is beautiful and stubborn, but I do not want her. But I fear that it might be too late for me."

"I understand." And he did. Riss had a feeling that they would be lucky if they made it to days end before Agon kissed her. And less than a week before he was bedding her. Riss wondered if there was a feather or two in the front room of the house he could lay upon Judith's bed. Leaving his friend, he went to find one. It would be worth it to know that Agon was as happy as he was.

Chapter 3

Judith was very good at ignoring things that she didn't want to see, like the man that sat on her counter as if he had nothing better to do with his time than to watch her every move. But the other man, Agon, was driving her crazy. He'd been in her room when she'd awoken and had followed her around like a wounded puppy all morning. Then about an hour ago, the other man had shown up, telling her he was her protector for the rest of her days. He'd kept his distance, but she knew that he'd be leaving her, too. She didn't want anyone around her. The fucking people were driving her insane. Why didn't anyone listen to what she wanted? Why did everyone think they knew her better than she did herself? So she did what she did best, ignored them in favor of working.

The jams were setting up nicely. She wanted them to be perfect, and adding just a touch of cherry juice to the strawberries had given them a lovely color. Glancing at the crates of blackberries that had been brought to her that morning, she was excited about getting started on them as well. She moved to the pot on the stove to see how the soap was coming along. She loved the smell of the pink flowers she'd found in the wooded area yesterday.

"What is the difference between jam and jelly?" Her assistant, Jane Holloway, a young girl from the local college, looked at her. "Jam and jelly. What's the difference?"

As with all people, Judith had avoided touching the young girl. They had come close a few times, but she'd managed in the three weeks that Jane had been coming to help her not to touch even her clothing. But lately, like today, it seemed as if Jane had it in her head to touch her, and Judith was getting annoyed by it.

Judith tried to think of her question and when she remembered, she nodded toward what she'd been working on. Keeping her distance, she explained the differences.

"Jelly is made from fruit juice; jam is made from the pulp of juice, or sometimes simply crushed fruit. And preserves, which I also make, has chunks of fruit in it, like whole strawberries or other fruits." Judith picked up the jam that was cool now and set the small jar on the window shelf. She set the other two kinds, all strawberry, on the same shelf. "See the difference?"

Agon came up behind her and looked, too. She wanted to scream at him to back off, but she had figured out earlier that no one could see the two men but her. Not even Benny had remarked on them when he'd come by an hour ago to ask her a few more questions. Instead of asking Agon to move, she backed into him to get him to move out of her bubble, the area she claimed as her own. It was a mistake, and she knew it the moment he wrapped his arm around her waist.

"You smell like your jams." His breath, like his words, fanned over her neck when he spoke near her ear. "I would very much like to see if you taste as good as I believe you would. For as much as I do not want a wife, the thought of tasting every part of you has me wanting more."

Moving away from him was the hardest thing she'd ever done in her life. He didn't pull her back to him, which surprised her. Men, in her experience, did not give up so easily. She wondered if this was some sort of trick he was playing on her just to throw her off. Moving back to her stove, she stirred the kettles as she tried her best to get control of herself.

They worked until just after two. Jane had a class and needed to be there. After a lengthy conversation with the other man, Agon sat down on the counter and the other man left. She had to take several deep breaths when she nearly messed up measuring the sugar three times.

"I could help you." She didn't answer him. It had worked before, ignoring the men who were there to watch her. But she had a deep feeling that Agon wasn't going to be easily dissuaded. "It is customary to answer someone when they speak to you, is it not?"

"Not when you don't want them here." She poured the sugar into the pot and looked at him. "Why don't you just leave? I don't want you here. And in the event you didn't notice, there was someone else sent here to watch over me."

"He will not be coming back." She looked at Agon when he hopped off the counter and came near her. She moved back when he was entering her space, and he stopped. "I will not harm you."

"So I've been told before. I'd very much like it if you would go back over there. I don't want you near me." He nodded but didn't move. "Whatever is going through your mind right now is not—"

"What does it feel like to kiss? I mean, to kiss a woman that has lips that seem to call to you, with a scent that no other human has but you? Will you taste of the berries you have eaten as you work? Will you be all the sweeter for them? Or will you taste of honey, the sweetest thing I have ever had the pleasure of eating?" She felt her breath leave her body at his question. "I have seen it done many times in all my life, but have never wanted to...I would imagine that it would take two people to kiss, would it not? Would you help me with my questions, Judith? Help me to see what it is that calls to me so loudly?"

"This isn't a good idea. You and I both know it. Are you telling me you've never kissed anyone?" He nodded and smiled at her. "I don't believe you. A man that looks like you, and you're telling me you've never been kissed? I suppose next you'll tell me you've never had sex either."

"I have not." She backed up when he took a small step toward her. "It is forbidden. Kissing as well as sex. But I'm finding it very difficult to think of anything else but sex with you, and kissing. I should very much like to have both with you."

"No." Her voice sounded breathless, and she thought he knew it. Judith cleared her throat and tried again. "I'm not having sex with you, and you are not going to kiss me. I don't know what kind of person you think I am, but I don't have sex with strangers. So you just back the fuck up and go over there where you were. If you're not going to leave, then you should stay back so I can—"

"I am no stranger to you." She felt her body respond to his closeness as he took another step toward her. As hard as she tried, she could not back up. Her body had a mind of its own right now and she was so fucked. "Just a kiss. I would very much like a single kiss to see if you are as delicious as I believe you to be."

She wanted him to touch her. It scared her in ways she didn't understand, yet she wanted it. When he cupped the back of her head and pulled her gently toward him, she went without any fight. As soon as his mouth brushed over hers, Judith moaned. He was going to hurt her, she just knew it.

As far as kisses went, it was quick. His mouth was firm and soft at the same time, yet she found she wanted more. Before he pulled completely back from her, Judith suckled his lower lip into her mouth and nipped at him. He groaned and pulled her body to his.

"Do it again. Touch your mouth to mine again and open your mouth." She put her hand on his chest as he did as she asked. "Kiss me, Agon. Taste me please."

His mouth took her with so much hunger this time that she had to hold onto him or fall. Judith slid her tongue along his and gripped harder on his arm so she wouldn't drag him to her bed, because she was sure that was where this was going to end. The man may not have any experience at this, but he certainly caught on quickly. He made love to her mouth like she wanted him to do to her body. As he slid his leg between hers, she felt his cock as he rocked against her. Tearing his mouth from hers, he looked down at her.

"My cock aches." She nodded and pulled him down to her mouth again. He cupped her ass and brought her closer to him, and she felt her body heat up with need. "Tell me what I should do. I need…I need some relief. You will help me, yes? You'll give me what I need, what we both need, please?"

She did need it as well, and if he kept rocking into her pussy like he was, she was going to get it. He was taking her so close to the edge that she knew that once she tumbled, there would never be any way she could get rid of him. Cupping his balls, she cried out when he nipped at her throat. Her climax was so close that she could feel it in her entire body. But a sound, hard and pounding, had her pulled from him and behind him before she could come. The door opened before she could think, and she was shoved away just as someone stepped into the room.

"Why are you here?"

Judith didn't move from behind Agon but stood there trying to catch her breath as he spoke to the newcomer. She'd been so close, her body primed for her climax, that she'd completely forgotten she didn't want him near her. When he asked the question again, she walked from behind his wings and looked at the man standing there. He looked...he looked like he was going to bust from laughter.

"I have just come from a visit with Joseph. He said that you dismissed him. I thought...I assumed you did not want to be here." Judith watched as the man took a step in her direction and Agon's wings spread more. "You think to protect her from Me, Agon?"

"I do not...she is mine to protect." The man nodded and looked at her. "She was just explaining a kiss to me. It is not...it is something that I have never experienced before. And she was nice enough to show me how it was done."

Judith wasn't sure she liked the way the other man smiled at her, but she was too hurt by what Agon was saying to give it much thought. She felt dismissed for some reason.

"Yes. I saw that." His laughter made her think he didn't do it often, and she took another step from Agon. Whoever this man was he was making fun of her, and she didn't much care for that either.

"He asked you a question. What are you doing here?" He raised a brow at her, and she felt embarrassed. Stiffening her spine, she glared at him. "I have had more people in and out of my life in the past few days than I have in years. I want you to get out. Both of you. I don't want anyone around me. Ever. And as for teaching you how to kiss? You're pretty good, but I don't want you to touch me again. I've things to do."

"I am not going to leave you." Agon took a step toward her, and she backed up. "You must not be afraid of me. I will never...I will never harm you."

"So you keep telling me." She looked at the other man. "Who are you and what are you doing in my shop? For that matter, how the hell did you get in here?"

"I appeared." She shook her head, trying to clear out some more of the sexual haze she'd been in when the man sat. "You are much stronger than I first thought. I do believe you will be good for My Agon. He needs you."

"But I don't need him." She moved to the door and opened it. "It's time for you both to get out of here. I've work to do and you are keeping me from it." The man stood up and moved toward the door. He looked back at Agon, who looked as if he wanted to argue, but he moved toward the door as well. Judith had no idea why she thought so, but she knew that the man was somehow boss to Agon. When they were both out the door, she locked it again and stood leaning against it. Judith was in so much trouble that she wanted to sit in the corner and cry.

~~~

"I believe you were told to stay away from her." Agon nodded but said nothing. The fact that she was alone was all he could think about, and he wanted to explore more of what she'd shown him in her shop. "Agon, are you listening to me?"

"Yes, my Lord, I am." He sat down in the chair across from His desk and looked at his boss. The man had been...He'd been forever, and His rules and laws had been something that Agon and the others had followed their entire lives. And now all Agon could think about was defying Him.

"Well, it did not look as if you were doing that when I saw you just now." Agon flushed, and his face heated up from what he'd been doing to Judith when Boss had spoken. "What do you have to say for yourself?"

"I simply wanted a kiss." Boss leaned back in His chair but said nothing. "She does not taste like I had thought a woman would. I thought...I have no idea what I thought, but she tastes like you might have used her taste to create some of the wondrous things here. And the glorious way her body fit to mine made me want to toss her upon her table and take her."

"You did not look as if you were taking a simple taste, Agon. You looked as if you were just short of taking her against the table, as you have said. She is your charge and you have said many times, I might add, that you have no desire to have her." Boss laughed and Agon felt an emotion surge up from nowhere. He had no idea what it was, but he wanted to harm the man in front of him because of it. "I would not do it if I were you. It will do you more harm than you can heal from. And in the event you do not know the emotion you are feeling, it's called jealousy."

"She is mine." Boss nodded, and Agon got up to pace. "I have been tricked into wanting her. I told Michael that I never wanted a female and now he has put one in front of me like a carrot. That is not fair."

"Fair or not, you were told that you were to stay away from her. If he did dangle a carrot like her in front of you, it would have been simple for you to stay away. Yet you have made it so that no one else can go near her, and you have kissed her as well. That does not sound like a man who does not want a female. This female in particular."

Agon knew what He was saying was correct. He'd been warned numerous times to back off, mostly by her, but it was…. There was something about her that he'd never felt with a woman before. And he was afraid of what Riss had told him, that she would be like nothing he'd ever felt before. He had to stay away or end up with not only a female in his bed, but one that made him think things he'd never thought of before.

"I wish for you to send Joseph back to watch over her. I will stay…I will try to stay away from her." Agon rubbed the sudden pain in his heart. "She will be happier this way, and I will not have her temptation so close at hand. It would be better for all of us if he were to be her watcher."

He left the office to go to his room when Boss agreed. Agon had a feeling he was making the biggest mistake of his life. As he lay on his bed, he thought about her touch, the way her body had felt so close to his, and he felt his cock stretch again. He knew that it was sexual and that being with her would give him the relief he needed, but it would only be for a brief time. But if he took her in any way, he'd be with her for the rest of his life, and that was something that just could not be. Agon rolled over and closed his eyes. Sleep took him almost immediately.

The pain in his body woke him with a start. Agon sat up and ran his hand over his entire self, wondering if he had somehow been harmed while he slept. His cock, hard as stone now, cramped again, and he knew it was Judith. Sitting up, he moved to the portal that would lead him to Riss's home, and detoured at the last moment to simply check on Judith. Or at least that was what he kept telling himself. It was a lie, and he knew it.

She was in her bed, but she was writhing and moving in a way that made Agon want to join her. There was a small vibrating sound coming from her, and he stepped closer to see what it could be. As soon as she saw him, Agon felt if he did not free his cock now, he would injure himself.

"I need to come." He nodded, not having a clue what she meant. "I need to climax, to come hard. Will you help me? This is all your fault anyway."

"My fault? I do not—" The sheet that had been covering her was tossed aside and he looked down at her naked body. Agon swallowed twice before he thought he could speak. "You are lovely."

"Come here." He nodded and moved the last few feet to her. "Take off your clothes. You're going to get a quick, hard lesson in sex and give me what I need at the same time."

He pulled his shirt over his head and dropped it to the floor. He would help her in any way that he could so long as she did not cover herself again. When she reached for his pants, pulling them open in such a violent way that his zipper snapped, Agon nearly told her he could do it. But she took his cock into her mouth, and he cried out.

He felt his balls tighten and his hips surged forward of their own accord. Agon rocked into her mouth over and over as she wrapped her hand around his shaft and pumped him. He had never felt anything like this before. And when she pulled away, he whimpered.

"Fuck me." He had no idea what she wanted but nodded again. He was beginning to feel like a simpleton when she lay back on the bed and spread her legs. Her womanhood was there for him to see, and he felt his mouth water to have a taste of her. When her fingers slid into her curls, Agon dropped to his knees. He would not have been able to stand on his own for much longer, and this was the safest way for him not to fall upon her. And that made his cock ache more.

"I need to come. Come and eat me. Please? I'm not getting any relief from Bob." Agon looked around the room for this Bob person, and she shoved a large vibrating cock at him. He looked at it, then at her. "Use it on me or eat me. Either way, I need your help."

Eating her sounded good. But he wasn't sure what he was supposed to be doing when he saw how wet her fingers were and the vibrating cock. He wondered if she had—

"You wish for me to use this inside of you?" Her nod made him flush. "In your womanhood?"

"Please, yes. Or your mouth. Take my pussy into your mouth and make me come." He leaned forward before he could think about what he should be doing, and her fingers curled into his hair. Before he knew it, he was buried in her soft curls, and her scent made him want to drink from her.

Licking her made his cock throb. Wrapping his fingers around himself to ease the pain, he licked her again and again until he felt a hard nubbin. When he nipped at this part of her, she cried out and flooded his mouth with more of her creamy juices. Agon spread her wider with his fingers and feasted on what she was offering him. He knew as surely as he was drinking from her that this was going to be the end of things as he knew them. And at that very moment, he did not care.

Nothing had ever tasted so delicious to him, and he had a feeling that it never would again. Every swipe of his tongue gave him more and more of her until he slid his tongue into her opening. Her body nearly bucked him off, but he knew it was not from pain but incredible pleasure. The more of her he took into him, the more he wanted of her. When she lifted his head, begging him to take her, Agon looked at his cock.

"I am leaking." She sat up and reached for him, wrapping her fingers around him again and sliding her hand up and down. "That feels very good. I should like to have relief as well, I think."

"Come up on the bed and I'll ride you." He nodded and stood up. He wasn't sure what she was going to do to him, but whatever it was, he knew that he would enjoy it. When she had him laying back on the bed, his cock stretched from him and he was embarrassed for himself. Cupping his cock into his hands, he was embarrassed at his size and the fact that he'd been leaking so profusely that he was sticky with it. But she pulled his hands away and put her mouth to him again.

Agon felt his balls tighten again, and he held her to him as she licked his length. This time when she stopped, he begged her to please do it again. Something profound was going to happen, but not if she kept pulling away from him.

When she straddled his hips, he sat up, only to be pushed back down. He held his cock when she instructed him to, and watched as she lowered her womanhood over him. Agon felt his eyes roll to the back of his head when she was seated over him.

"You are tight around me. And I am deep within you." She nodded and moved her hips forward and back. "Yes. That's wonderful. More. I need more."

Agon gripped her hips…to hang on, he told himself. But he thought it was more like he didn't want her to stop. If she did that now, he wasn't sure he would survive it. Her body moved over his in waves, making him think of the tides being pulled by the moon. As she cupped her breasts and rolled her nipples, Agon sat up and took the hard morsels into his mouth and suckled. Judith cried out when he nipped.

"Again." She held him to her, and he cupped the other breast, doing what she had done with her nipples. Her rolling hips seemed to have gotten out of rhythm a little, and he rolled her to her back and moved his cock, something that felt better than he could ever imagine, into her heat. When she wrapped her ankles around him, Agon pumped into her as hard as he could. And when she tightened around him, screaming out his name, Agon felt his body release inside of her.

He pumped more and more, bringing her to peak twice more before he spilled his seed within her. Dropping upon her, he rolled to his back so as not to hurt her with his weight, taking her with him. Agon could not speak, could hardly breathe, and knew that whatever he'd thought before about sex with this woman was as wrong as it could ever be.

"You're going to hate me in the morning." He lifted her chin when she spoke, and he frowned at her. "You will. You're going to be in deep shit with that other guy, and when he finds out we just had sex, he's going to hit the roof."

"I do not believe this was just sex. It was much too wonderful to have such a lazy term attached to it." She giggled, and he tightened his grip on her back to bring her closer to him. "As for Boss? I am not sure He will hit the roof either. He will be most displeased with me, yes, but He is not one to have fits of anger. At least not in a long while He has not."

She sat up and rested her chin on her fist as she looked at him. "I'm not...we can't do this again. First of all, we didn't use any protection and I don't do that sort of sex. And...and this is really important for you to understand. I don't want you in my life. I have things just the way I want them, and having you here will mess them up."

He tried his best not to be hurt by her words, but he was. He knew that he'd been saying the same to her, but for some reason, he felt as if things were changed now. Instead of telling her he was not leaving her, not after this, he pulled her back to his chest and held her. He knew the moment she was asleep, and he pulled her tighter to his heart, a place he was sure she was always meant to be.

Agon reached for Michael to tell him what he'd done. The man laughed for so long that Agon wanted to go to the realm and hit him. When he finally calmed enough for Agon to continue, Michael laughed again.

I do not think this is funny. You have put her before me. What did you think would happen when you did this? He pulled Judith closer to his body when she shivered. *I would think you'd be happy but not find this humorous. You are making a fool of yourself. Are you aware of that?*

That I am, but I find that I do not care. I am happy, my good man, but I didn't think it…well, I thought she would hold out longer. You must have used some powerful magic on her to get her—

I did no such thing. I was…she was doing things to herself that…I will not discuss this with you if you continue to laugh. Michael's laughter was something that was often heard but rarely directed at anyone but himself. To be laughed at by this man, this great man, had Agon both pleased and embarrassed. When Michael stopped laughing again, he spoke, but with a great deal of humor still bubbling forth.

Boss will need to speak to you both before long. I will set it up with Him to have a meeting. He will be pleased that you are happy. Agon wasn't sure he was happy so much as he was sated, and said as much to the man. *You are happy. I would imagine that you have her wrapped in your wings now and have her safely cocooned close to you.*

He did. And he had not realized he'd done so until Michael mentioned it. To have her wrapped into his wings and feel so good about it made his heart sing with newfound happiness. He pulled them tighter around them as he spoke to Michael.

I will be watching her now. I do not want others to be near her. Michael agreed. *And we must work hard to find out who would try to harm her. The men with the bullets gave no clue as to why they came for her.*

She knows. Agon looked at Judith. She knew? He started to ask Michael what she knew when he spoke first. *I must go. I have two meetings that I cannot miss. There are still things that must be covered and I have to go to the training area at noon. I would like to see you both there as well.*

Agon laid there for several hours before sleep claimed him as well. He had many questions to ask Judith when she woke, and he wanted to tell her that he was not leaving her. Agon also wondered if he would be able to taste her once again before he left her bed.

Chapter 4

"You should have seen it. Wings. I fucking tell you, that man had wings." Jerry tried to ignore the man who had been babbling in front of him for the past hour, but it was becoming more and more difficult. He had to be high as well. A man with wings indeed.

"And you say that he saved her. While three of my best men were shot to death, a winged man leapt in and saved her. And shall we discuss again how I said to bring her in, not shoot her up full of holes to the point where I cannot use her? What is it you're smoking? Whatever it is, I want to market it. There is no fucking way you are simply high on the shit I sell."

Chad sat down and glared, but he didn't mention the winged man again. "I have another crew going out there again today. I also have one that works with her. She said the woman just works at the house and makes jelly and shit."

Jerry knew that more than anyone. He'd been trying to get her to come to him for years and she simply wouldn't let go of her little piece of property and come and work for him, giving it all to him. He didn't need it, but the nice little building she'd put up would have a nice little operation in it before she was settled in her room…a locked room. It was in a prime neighborhood, and he wanted that little corner more than he wanted anything else. Not to mention the girl who lived there.

Judith Craft was his niece. Very few people knew about their relationship, and fewer still knew that his brother and he had gone to great lengths to try and get the little bitch to help them out on a few deals. Now that his brother was filling the belly of a few worms, he felt it was his duty to go and bring the girl into his fold, so to speak. Judith had a gift he was planning to capitalize on, and very nicely, too…the fact that she could touch a man and tell them where he had been and what he'd been up to. And, well, Jerry was going to be very, very wealthy when it was all said and done.

"Find a way to bring her to me, and unharmed. If she has so much as a hair out of place, I will make sure that you pay for it. I'm not shitting you when I tell you I do not want her harmed in any way." Chad mumbled something, and Jerry picked up his gun and pointed it at him. "Repeat yourself."

"I said I told them not to shoot the place up, only to make her go out the back so we could nab her back there. But we couldn't get in. That damned fence she had running around her property has enough juice running through it that it damned near took off Jobs hand when he touched it." Chad sat up more in his chair. "That guy we walked in on while we was there, he never said a word about no electric fencing. And it wasn't what we'd meant to do by killing him. Jobs thought he was reaching for a gun."

"Walked in on?" Chad nodded. "You killed a man? When? And why wasn't I made aware of this before now?"

"Some dude was picking up some of her jelly or some shit. He was putting the boxes in his car and we startled him like. I never knew a man as big as he was could scoot like that. Startled Jobs enough that he drew and fired before we could hide out." Jerry washed his hand over his face and looked at his gun. The temptation to shoot this man was overwhelming, and if he didn't need him, he might just have done it. Putting the gun down, he stared at Chad.

"You are, by and large, the stupidest man I've ever known. No. Stop that. You are the stupidest man ever born. Why are you going into the house, shooting a man, and not coming out with the girl I want?" Chad shrugged. "That is not an answer. Tell me."

"I got the hell outta there before we was caught. Turns out I was right. The rest of them are dead and I'm not." Jerry eyed the gun again but left it while Chad continued. "I'll get her tomorrow. I swear it. Or the next day."

After he left, Jerry picked up the gun and put it back in his drawer. He was never sure when he might need it, and didn't want to take the chance of someone knowing it was there and taking it from him. As much time as he'd spent in prison, he was not going back because someone had gotten a burr up their ass about him owning a gun.

Prison. He rarely thought of it anymore. He'd been there for nearly twelve years before he was able to work the system in his favor. Not that he wasn't still working the system, but now he was doing it from the comfort of his own home and not behind bars. And he had his pretty little niece to thank for his confinement.

"Sir, there's a call for you on line three. It's the commissioner." Jerry rolled his eyes, wondering what the hell the man wanted now. If he asked him for another dime, Jerry was going to take him out of the office he had coveted so badly and put him next to his brother, Lindale. Enough was enough, for Christ's sake.

"I've just been informed that it was your hoods that shot up the jelly house on Third." Jerry sat up, wondering how the hell the dots had connected to him. "Next time you send in idiots to kill someone, make sure they don't have your fucking business cards in their pockets. The fucking feds are all over this one now."

"Make it go away." Commissioner Bonds snorted, then started speaking about how he had no way of doing this and blah blah blah. "I don't want to hear why you can't do it. I said to make it go away. I have more important things to do than to babysit you. And if I have to, then I might as well put someone in your place."

"You wouldn't." Jerry didn't bother answering because he most certainly would and Bonds knew it. "I'll do what I can. But I'm telling you now, they want your ass more than you do your next breath."

After he hung up on the man, Jerry leaned back in his seat. It was time to put the man out to pasture. Commissioner Bonds had outlived his usefulness as of that moment. After a few more phone calls, it was settled. Peter Bonds was going to contract an unfortunate illness that he'd never recover from.

Jerry smiled as he made his way to his car at the end of his workday. All four hours of it. Soon now he'd have Judith in his hands, and all her information was going to be his. And he planned to make good use of her, too. He'd bet any amount of money the girl would fetch a high price from some of his buddies to get the chance to fuck the little piece of ass. Even a few women he knew, as well. But it was her talent that he wanted first and foremost.

His brother had told him that his daughter was a freak when she'd been a child. He'd never really taken it very seriously, as Lindale was forever calling someone a freak. But the first time he'd seen her do her thing, he knew that his brother didn't see the big picture of things. Judith and her ability were going to make them rich, at least until he could have figured out a way to get Judith into his hands. Then it would have been all his. But he'd killed Lindale before he had a plan for someone else to take the fall.

Judith had been sitting at the table when he'd been visiting one morning, and he sat beside her. Judith had never taken to him. When he'd figured out why, he would go out of his way to crowd her, going so far as to hug her to him when he was near enough to touch her. But on that particular day, she'd turned to him and spoken of things he'd long since forgotten.

"There are seven men buried on your property. Five of them you shot yourself. The others by men who work for you. Not that it matters. You were the one who ordered the trigger to be pulled, so it's all you. Each of them owed you something. Not money, because you think you have more than you can spend, but they had territories that you wanted. Drug land, you call it, because it sounds so much like an amusement park. Three of the men are buried near the pool, one under the pool house, and two out in a pasture where you have cows that you never look at." He looked around the room and stared at his brother as Judith continued. "You want to kill my dad because you think he won't give me to you. You think he wastes my talent, as you call it, and you want to profit from me. But I have news for you. I'd rather die than help you. And you will die, too. Would you like to know when?"

"She's lying." As Jerry denied what she said, Lindale shook his head and moved back from his daughter as if she were something he should be afraid of. Perhaps he was afraid of his little monster. The gun in his hand hung limply by his side, but he had his finger in the trigger guard. "Lindale, you have to know that I'd never kill you. And what nonsense is she talking about, using her for her talent? What have you been telling her?"

"He doesn't have to tell me anything you do with every part of yourself. You touched me and opened your lies to me." He backhanded her off the couch and looked at his brother as she lay there limp as a rug.

"Lindale, I'd never—" To this day, Jerry wasn't sure who had fired first. But when it was over, he'd gone to prison for killing his brother. Judith testified against him and he'd wanted to exact his revenge on her since then. Prison had not been anything he felt he deserved for defending himself. But the girl was going to work for him, and then he was going to bury her in the fucking fields without so much as a marker to show she'd ever been a part of this earth.

~~~

Boss stood up when Judith entered the room. She stilled for several seconds before she moved into the room and headed for the refrigerator. He waited until she sat down before He spoke.

"I would like to talk to you." She looked up from her bowl of colorful cereal before dropping her head back down to her chore. "It's important that you understand what is—"

"I don't care." He nodded. And as much as He knew this was going to be painful for them both, He had to talk to her. "I've told you since...you came to me before and I told you then not to come back. It was a long time ago, but you were there. So, if you think that you have more to say to me, then I'd just as soon you kept your mouth shut."

"It was already in the works before he was killed." He wanted to reach for her but knew of all His creatures, she was the one He could not reach. Not yet at any rate. "I only meant to keep you safe. Had things not progressed as they had, then—"

"You mean killing my father was somehow in this grand plan you have?" He nodded. "I suppose you're going to tell me that had this not happened, I'd be dead now and not a part of your little scheme to get Agon a wife. Which, I would like to point out, is not going to happen."

"You'll not marry him?" She got up and dumped her bowl into the sink. As she started to leave the room and Him, He stood up and spoke. "He will die if you do not."

She paused and He had a hopeful moment, hoping that she would be reasonable and listen to Him. Then she turned to Him, and Boss could see the pain in her face; her heart was breaking and He had caused it. Boss took a step toward her only to be brought up short when she backed away.

"He'll go back with you today. Don't allow him to return. If you do, then I will...I'll...I will end my own life. You know I will, and this time no one will find me until it's too late." He'd nearly been too late before. "Do you understand me?"

"Yes." He took the step toward her, and she held her ground. "But when he comes to you, and he will, what will you do then? Shove him out of your heart, too? Make him suffer for caring about you? Or will you have him there to watch you die? He won't leave you, no matter what I tell him. You have taken his heart and he will not let you go."

"See that he does." She was gone before Boss could say anything else. He wasn't sure what He might have said to her, but He sat back down. When Agon appeared in the room a few minutes later, He asked him to have a seat.

"She does not want you here." Agon stood up, only to sit when He asked him to. "I must tell you everything. Judith is...she will not...I'm not sure where to begin. I suppose at the start would help."

Agon nodded.

"She was born to a mother who was clinically dead. They kept her alive so that Judith, only about five months old in the womb, would have a better chance to survive. I visited them both often and helped more than I should have to keep the babe alive. And because of the way she was helped, her abilities—her horrors, as she calls them—were something that came because of what I did to keep her safe."

"She is blessed." Boss shrugged. "I know that she does not see it that way, but she has been. You saved her for me. You knew that we would be a couple, a single being."

"I did." Boss touched Agon's hand and they went to His office. There He brought up the day that Judith took her first breath. "From the start she was special. Nurses could see it. Her time in the nursery was spent quietly. No one bothered her until her father, his grief profound, came for her. She never caused him any problems, but he began to hate her."

Fast forwarding to her early years, Boss paused a few times to show the father ignoring his little girl in favor of the drugs he took. Medicine he called it. But Judith had known, even as a small child, that it was more than that. It was what took him from her.

"When it became apparent that she was different, he worked hard to get her to not show off. Not allow others to see what she could do. At first it was the simple things…moving a cup to her, lifting a book from a shelf far across the room. Then Judith showed him that she could find out things from other people. That was when he decided that he could profit from her. A drug deal going down or money left somewhere that would be retrieved later. A robbery from a store, and it would happen so he could be there when the thief came out, to take from him what he'd stolen. All things he could be there to get the cash, or in some cases, the drugs to sell for even more money." Boss stopped the pictures — memories of her at one place — and didn't speak as He and Agon looked at the child.

She'd been put into a cage, an animal cage that was much too small for her, and left there without a blanket or food for two days. He moved on before stopping at yet other picture of her tied to her bed, and a slice of bread nearby that looked moldy and hard. When Agon spoke from behind Him, Boss turned and saw the tears on his cheeks.

"No one ever cared for her." Boss nodded, then shook His head. "How did we allow this to happen? Why did her protector not help her somehow?"

"He did all he could. But she ignored him for the most part. Her father told her she was insane for believing in us, and he beat her more when she mentioned when someone came to her." Agon nodded and sat down. "She soon began to see us not as a protector but as someone who would cause her pain."

"I heard her this morning. She said she would kill herself if I returned to her. I don't know what to do." He looked at Him, and Boss had a feeling Agon didn't want to hear what He had to say but would ask anyway. "Tell me how to save her."

"You must not give her a chance to push you away." He looked at the stilled picture of her seemingly looking at a camera. He knew that she'd seen Him there...she'd always known about Him and the others. "Her path will only grow if you are with her. She will...you both will suffer if she is not with you when her uncle comes for her."

"Uncle?" Boss nodded at Agon and showed him what the man looked like. "He wants to cause her harm? He is her only living relative then? And he wishes to hurt her? He should be caring for her, loving her."

"He is a man with his own agenda, I fear. One that would have her dead before her time. A man without any dogmas or heart when it comes to getting back what he feels she owes him. He will kill her." Agon sat down and stared at the man. A man who would not just kill Judith but take Agon as well.

Agon left Him a while later. Boss moved back to the memories and moved beyond what was to what would be. He knew better than anyone that courses could be changed, but he knew the outcome of all. Stopping at the point where things would go either way for the couple, He smiled at the look she had on her face.

"You will someday tell Me you love Me, My child. And when you do, I shall give you all that you want.

Agon will care for you, love you very much, but it will be Me that cares for you for all your lives." He left His offices to go to find Michael. Tomorrow was the beginning of the end for the couple, and He wanted to make sure things were in line.

"I do not understand this." Boss nodded after talking to Michael for twenty minutes, but he was coming around finally. "You wish for me to make sure that Agon is busy elsewhere when she needs him most?"

"She will need him, but must ask. He will…it will be for the best." Michael cocked a brow at Him. "I do have some tricks up my sleeve. You will please do this because I have said so."

"You are talking about the same woman I am, correct? The one that just today had a fight with Agon that several other protectors came to watch? She is…I was going to say vocal, but I've come to realize just now that she is a great deal like you. I believe she would say it was raining if she were standing in a sunny field." Boss laughed, and Michael growled. "It was not meant to be a compliment. I was trying to make a good point."

"But it was a compliment to me, don't you see? Now. Are we clear on what will happen?" Michael nodded and huffed at him. "It will not be so bad. Once she says his name, things will fall into place. You will say I was right when this is over, I think."

"You are forever right, so that will not be difficult for me to do. I do, however, want to point out that she will not be happy with anyone when she finds out what we have done." Boss nodded and figured she'd be screaming at Him soon. "I will not take responsibility for her actions if she finds You. And I have a feeling that she will find

You and You will allow her to. You like a good fight as much as she does."

"Yes I do. So few people will stand up to Me, including you, but I think she gives as good as she gets. Our conversations are lively, I think. But I will take it all upon myself when she is upset." Boss mentally rubbed His hands together. He needed a good sparring partner and knew that Judith would be it. Kala was getting much too cranky in her later blooming, but He knew that while Judith and Agon would...well, He was looking forward to this round. And He might even let her think she'd won, for a while anyway.

Boss made His way to Riss and the compound. He wanted to see the work that was going on, and mayhap He'd find a minute or two to play the new game that the men had invented. It was something that Riss had made up in his long hours of watching the worms so long ago.

There were nine men and women in the building. Boss stayed in the back, as far from the others as He could get while He watched. The name of the exercise was Dutiful, and the rules were simple...stay focused.

"There are over ten million dots on this wall. All of them are black and all but one is round. You have three minutes to find the one that is not." The protectors came up in pairs and searched and searched without any luck. Finally when they had all had a turn, Riss looked at Him. "Do you see it?"

"Nay, I do not." He got up to look at the board and searched as hard as the others. Finally He turned and looked at Riss. "There is not one, is there?

For an answer, Riss pointed to the first dot. It was square, not round. And once He saw it, He could pick it out in seconds. When the board was changed, He was able to find it immediately. He looked at Riss. This plan, or whatever it was, made no sense to Him or the others just yet.

"You were expecting something else the first time you looked, correct? Not sure what, but each person here knew what the odd dot would look like in their mind. But once you knew what to see, then finding it was easy. It's the same with the humans we watch. Day after day we see them, and day after day we see the changes. Some of them are small; others large. Then there are the changes we cannot see, but which make us look all the harder for them. Changes such as moods and temperaments. But sometimes looking hard is not what we need to do. It's looking for the simple things, like an odd dot, that will make us better protectors." Riss smiled. "It is why we are there for them. Before anyone else, we can see their dots or squares because we have looked daily. Any change will stand out quicker because we watch. That is why we must remain, above all else, Dutiful."

After a few more lessons on paying attention, He left the building. He'd found what He'd wanted. The protectors were more relaxed than they had been in months, some of them decades, and He could see smiles and hear laughter that had been long in coming.

There were men and woman on the track as well. Most of them were in pairs, but some ran alone. It wasn't just a way to stay fit but a way for them to unwind, and to be free of any worries. There were none of those here, it seemed. It was just as He'd planned. A place for them to regroup and to smile. Boss watched them for a few minutes more before He made his way to the other fields. Things were progressing nicely.

"You should go and see the pool that's being put in." Boss turned to look at Kala when she came toward Him. "It's much bigger than I thought it would be. I was expecting something like the pool in town. This one is big enough to have the Olympics in." They made their way over to the area and He could see that it was only a day or so from being filled. "Will you use the pool when it's complete?"

"Mayhap." He watched for several minutes before He spoke again. "I should like your help. Judith is going to need a friend in the next week or so. I believe it would do her good for you to help her with finding a purpose."

"A purpose? You think what she does now isn't a purpose?" He started to speak, but she was on a roll and He let her go. "She makes the best jams and jellies I've ever eaten, and her soaps? I'm going to buy nothing else but that for the compound from now on. And her other herbs…did you know that you could cook with nearly everything in the ground, including grass?"

"I did." She huffed at Him, and Boss laughed. "I had a purpose, too, when I started out. I was merely asking that you give her a purpose with her selling her own products rather than selling them to others to resell. She has a shop front now, but it is small potatoes compared to what she could be doing. And another few employees to help her. It will do her good to see others. I think you would encourage her like none other."

"You knew that I'd go off on You, didn't You?" He laughed. "I think You enjoy arguing more than You do anything else."

"It does pass the time, my lady." She laughed with Him as they made their way to the house. "Will you see about helping her? It will not be easy, and may suit better if you were not to mention I asked you to help."

"Mad at You, is she? Well, she is under a lot of stress. What with living with a protector, keeping You out of her business, as well as someone trying to kill her." Boss nodded but said nothing. "I guess I'll have to see what I can do. And so you know, I'm counting on You to come to the pool opening. We're having food."

He told her He'd be there and left. Boss had a great deal of things going on and hadn't realized until He sat back at his desk how much He'd needed to simply get away. He might have to do this more often. Opening the computer He'd just had installed, He started making some changes to the other protectors He had on His list. It was going to be a very long time before He could get away again like He had today, but He would make the time from now on.

Chapter 5

Agon wasn't sure what to do. She had been not speaking to him for several hours now, and he was frustrated. Standing as close as he could to her without actually touching her, he felt her body stiffen. It was not what he wanted, but he wanted to make her feel him.

"I have been thinking of what transpired last night." She didn't say anything. "The love making. Have you ever...what I mean to say is...the thing that vibrated. Do you use it often?"

"When I need sex, I do. It's not often but sometimes I need to take the edge off. It works well for that. And unlike you, it's not annoying the morning after." She looked at him, and he had a feeling she was insulting him but only smiled. "And it doesn't crowd me. Will you please back the fuck up?"

"I think not." He moved his mouth over her neck and nipped gently at her shoulder. "I love the way you taste. Especially your womanhood. That was...I have never tasted anything so wonderful in my life. I'd very much like to do that again to you. To hear you scream out when you reach your peak. I don't think I've ever heard anything more amazing."

"No, I don't want you touching me again. You shouldn't even be here." He could feel her body stiffening more, but he felt it was due more to his words than her being mad. Wrapping his hands around her waist, he moved his hands up her belly to just under her breasts. Her breaths told him she was enjoying what he was doing. "You should get out of here now. I don't want you...please stop this."

"Your nipples are very hard. And the way that you moaned when I suckled them into my mouth made my cock very hard." He rocked into her bottom, and she moved back against him. Agon pressed into her until she was flush with the table she was working at. "If I were to take you this way, would you enjoy this? Would you scream out your release as you did last night?"

"I've never come that hard before."

He continued to rock back and forth into her bottom while he toyed with her breasts. When she leaned back into him, he lifted her shirt up and slid his hands under her bra to feel her warm flesh as it filled his hands. Her arms came up and over her head so that she could wrap her fingers into his hair.

"You're going to make me crazy with need. Why are you doing this?"

"I want to feel my body within yours again. Watch your face as you release. Did you know that your nipples flush when you are about to climax? That your body tightens around mine so tightly that I feel you ripple with your each enjoyment?"

She turned in his arms and took his mouth. Agon picked her up by her bottom, sat her on the counter, and tore her blouse open. He looked down at the bounty before him. She was magnificent.

"I should very much like to paint you this way. Flush with need that I have created, your body hard with your energy that you need to expel during release." Agon licked a path over her cupped breasts and flicked his tongue into her bra to taste the morsel there. "I should very much like to suckle you again."

He reached for the small closure at the front of her garment. It was foreign to him, but he soon figured it out. When he took the smallish hook from the loop, he watched her breathing pick up. Lifting the small piece of lace from her breast, Agon watched her face. He was amazed at the amount of emotion he could see there.

"You are so lovely." She licked her lips, and he needed to taste her. Licking his own tongue over her swollen lips, he moved back and looked at her nakedness. Agon leaned down and took the pert nipple into his mouth and nipped.

"I want to come." He didn't lift his head up until she pulled him up by his hair. "You need to help me come again. I need it."

"Do you need me or just the release?" She looked at him, then away, and he pulled her chin back around. "It is a simple question. One that I would very much like an answer for. I could go into your bedroom and retrieve the vibrating male phallus for you. Or do you need me?"

"Why are you doing this to me?" Agon didn't stop watching her face as tears started to stream down her cheeks. "I've been alone for a long time, not hurting anyone, not bothering them. Getting my own rocks off whenever I felt I needed it. Then you come along and now I can't stand the thought of going back to bed alone. That shouldn't happen after one night."

"But it has." She laid her head on his shoulder and sobbed. Agon lifted her into his arms and took her to the bedroom to lay her down. He wanted her no less than he did before, but somehow he knew that her heart would not be involved. He knew how much this had cost her, this confession that she needed him, and he simply wanted to hold her.

After seeing that she was comfortable, he lay beside her and held her to him. Agon ran his fingers up and down her spine, feeling her body relax by small degrees. When he was sure she was asleep, he held her just a bit longer before he reached for Michael.

I should like for you to tell Boss that I have failed Him again. I should...it will be necessary for me to end this life if Judith does not accept me as her husband. I know that I was warned about coming to her again, but I simply could not keep from her. Michael didn't say anything for several seconds, so Agon continued. *If you could see your way to letting me spend the final days here with her, I would very much appreciate it.*

Where are you going to stay, Agon? She has made it very clear that she does not want you there. Agon felt his heart twist and knew that Michael was right. She did not want him with her. *I can tell Him, but I don't know what He will say. I should hope that she'd take you, but her heart is hard to everyone.*

I understand. He lay there long after the sun set and morning began to crest in the sky. At just before dawn, he got out of the bed and looked down at her. Agon knew in that moment that he was in love with the woman. He kissed her cheek, covered her up, and left the house. It was time for him to come face to face with what he'd done.

~~~

Jerry was going to let the phone ring three more times before he hung up. What sort of business did his niece run that she wasn't there during normal business hours? And where was this woman that was working for him? He paid her good money. The fucking least she could do was answer the fucking phone. Chad hadn't been able to reach this…Jane Holloway, either. Not since his men had been killed at the shootout a few days ago.

"Hello." The snapped word made him want to go to the house and bitch slap the person. How rude did people have to be? "Are you there or not? I have shit to do, and waiting for you to get your shit together to answer me is fucking with my schedule."

"Judith?" Silence told him he had her. "It's your uncle. Uncle Jerry Craft. I was wondering if you have time to speak to me. It's a matter of some importance, and the sooner we get this conversation started, the sooner we can see things to their conclusion."

"No." He waited for her to explain or at least ask him what he wanted with her, but she said nothing else. Angry now, he sat up higher in his chair and let it go. He'd had enough shit going on today and dealing with her didn't put him in any better of a mood. So instead of doing what he'd wanted and try to woo her to him, he exploded at her.

"What the fuck is wrong with you? Don't you think…mother fuck, you're stupider than that halfwit of a father you had. I did you a favor by blowing his fucking brains out. I want you to get your ass here and talk to me. This bullshit has gone on long enough. You should have more respect for me. I'm your only living—"

"You're a real piece of work, aren't you? I'm not going to dignify that with any sort of comeback. Respect you?

Who the hell are you kidding? And you're my only living relative because you killed my father. And maybe you did do me a favor by killing him before he killed me, but I think you should be thanking me instead of the other way around. I probably saved you a lot of money on sex. Getting butt fucked must have done you a world of good." She laughed, a sound that reverberated into his skull like a jack hammer. "I hate you, and respect will never happen between us. So fuck the hell off, you mother fucking dick shit."

"You can't talk to me that way. I have your best interest at heart." She snorted at him, and he felt his temper get the better of him again. "Damn it all to hell and back. I demand that you come here at once. I've tried to be nice about it, but you continue to act as if I've done more to you than you deserve. Cut the shit, Judith, and get over here. I need you to do things for me. And if you need for me to try and make amends to get this shit settled, then so be it. But you're going to fucking owe me."

"Amends, huh? Is that why you sent four of your goons over here to kill me? Oh, and the one that got away, did he tell you that he hid around the corner like a scared little shit while his other men were blown away by the cops?" Jerry was going to have a little talk with Chad when he returned, but Judith continued before he could comment. "And what about the man who killed my coworker? Did you know that man had two children in college? How is that trying to make amends? Fuck your olive branch, you fucking murderer. I've told you this before, I don't want a thing to do with you. And if you come near me again, I will cause you a world of hurt."

"I would pay you for your services if that's what it'll take. Wouldn't you like to quit working in that sweat house all day and make some real money? And by real money, I'm talking millions. With a talent like yours, we could do so much together." He smiled when she didn't speak. He had her now. Money always did the talking with women like her. "I'm talking tens of millions of dollars. Money like that you can't make smashing up a bit of berries."

"No." He wondered if she was answering his statement about the amount of money she could make for him and continued. Jerry decided that he should have started off with talking about funding. Then he wouldn't have lost his temper.

"I'd give you twenty percent of the money we make off your information. I mean, the tracks alone would be worth a fortune to us. You go in and have a little talk with the horses and I'll lay the bets. Then I'd be taking you on some little meetings I have. You can tell me if so and so is planning to run over me or not. I think you just aren't seeing your full potential here, Judith. Think of all the possibilities we could get into, you and I. We'd make a wonderful team."

"Are you that stupid that you don't know what the word 'no' means? You just don't get it, do you? I don't want anything to do with you or that so-called business of yours." She laughed, and he had a memory of her father laughing the same way and felt a finger of fear run down his spine. "You are not going to be a part of my life. Not now, not ever. I don't need you or your fucking drug money. And keep that man away from me. If he comes here again, I will blow his fucking brains out. And while I know you don't give a fucking shit about his life, if I have to kill him, I'll make sure you go down for his murder."

The sound of the phone being disconnected shocked him. She'd actually hung up on him.

He was still holding the phone when Chad walked in. He was holding up a girl who looked like she was stoned out of her mind. When he shoved her into a chair, Jerry put the phone down.

"Meet Jane Holloway. She got a hold of your stuff and now look at her." Jerry reached into his drawer and pulled out his gun. Firing one shot at the girl, he hit her right between the eyes. She fell into the chair just as the blood splattered down the wall behind her. When he saw that she was indeed dead, Jerry aimed the gun at Chad. "What the fuck are you doing? You can't...mother fuck, you just fucking killed her."

"Yes, and you're next." The gun went off before Chad could say another word. Jerry knew the mess was going to be horrendous to clean up, but right then all he could think about was two less people to fuck up his day. He sat there staring at them until he had his temper under control. Now he had to go about the business of making sure that they would never be found. Mother fuck, could this day get any worse than it was right at that fucking minute?

He'd learned long ago, while in prison of all places, that cleaning up after yourself saved you a nice, long term behind bars or strapped to a chair while they filled you with lethal drugs to kill you. Two of his roomies had gone up because they'd trusted too easily. Hell, one of them even had their own brother turn them in when he'd buried a body for him. And Jerry had just the way to clean up after himself in the sublevels of his home.

He'd had the oversized kiln installed about a week after he'd gotten out of prison. Another mate had told him that he was going to burn the bodies and anything related to their deaths after he killed them. He'd told Jerry that even a fucking gun could be disposed of, just remember to take out the bullets before it was fired up. It was the reason he was sitting behind bars now. His fucking gun had gone off when the cops had come to ask him about a totally unrelated crime concerning his car. And an ex-con wasn't supposed to have any sort of firearm, and there he was with an entire kiln of them.

It was a little on the smelly side, his bunk mate had told him, much like a burning roast was. But it was a permanent way to dispose of all the evidence that would otherwise come back to haunt him. He moved to the lower levels of his house to get the necessary items to get rid of the two idiots.

It took him nearly three hours to get them to the basement, and another hour to figure out that he couldn't get them both in at the same time. He decided that he'd do the woman first, then Chad. He was stuffing her body into the kiln when he heard the doorbell ring. Moving through the basement to his computers, he was surprised to see who he thought was a cop standing on his doorstep. And he most assuredly didn't look happy to be there.

Jerry closed the lid of the kiln and decided that he'd wait to start it. No sense in having the cops smell what he was doing. Jerry was still laughing as he made his way to the front of the house. When he opened the door, he stared at the man standing there, not having a clue what to say. There was something about him that made Jerry's balls tighten to his body and his skin feel too tight.

"Jerry Craft?" He nodded before he could think maybe he shouldn't answer that. "My name is Michael. You and I have to have a conversation."

"Michael who?" The man shrugged, and Jerry frowned at him. "You won't tell me who you are, yet you expect me to allow you into my home. You're stupider than my ne...some other person I know if you think that I'm going to allow you to come in simply because you think I should." The man smiled, and Jerry took a step back. He was terrified, yet he had no idea why.

"I never asked for permission to enter. I simply asked if you were him and said that we needed to speak." Michael smiled. "It would be in your best interest for you to speak to me. I have a great deal of information about your future that you would need to know."

"I think not." Michael looked to his left, then back at him. Jerry looked as well, wondering if the man had someone hidden around the corner to attack when he let him in. But there was no one there, and he knew the man was off his rocker. "What the hell do you want?"

"Nothing from that area, I assure you." Jerry frowned again when Michael laughed. "I have simply come to speak to you about Judith. She and the rest of us would like for you to leave her alone. It would be in your best interest if you were to heed what I have to say to you. You may live longer, that's for sure."

"Leave her alone, you say? Are you by chance threatening me? I certainly hope the fuck you're not." Michael smiled but said nothing more. "And what business is this of yours what I may or may not be doing to my niece? You sleeping with her? Fucking her maybe? I'll have you know that she's not right in the head. Hasn't been since she was a kid."

"She's very well in the head, and no, I am not sleeping with her. She is not my wife. She is meant for another." Jerry wondered what that had to do with anything, but before he could ask, the man spoke again. "She is living with a man that means a great deal to me, and I'd very much like it if you would leave them in peace. Whatever you think you need from her will do you no good if you are caught harming her. There are others that are much stronger than you that would cause you a great deal of...harm."

"I'd never hurt her unless she tried something with me first." At least not right away, he thought. Jerry slipped his hand into his pocket to touch his gun and found it wasn't there. He tried to think where he'd left it and was coming up blank. Jerry wanted this guy gone so he could finish what he'd been doing and find his fucking gun. "You need to leave now."

"Your gun is in the lower levels with the two bodies you took there just before I arrived. I believe that I interrupted your working with them. It's a shame that you killed them, as they did very little to warrant your murdering them. But I suppose you are used to killing for pleasure. It is, from what I know of you, something that you do a great deal of the time instead of talking things out."

Jerry held onto the doorframe tighter but said nothing. How the hell did he know about...?

"You should also be aware that Judith has a good head on her shoulders and can locate any of the bodies you have killed regardless of what you might do with them in the kiln. They have records of such purchases as well. 'What would a man who has no artist ability want with something so expensive?' is what they will ask you just before they look into what you have been doing with it."

Jerry stood there for several seconds while the man smiled at him. He finally shut the door and leaned against it to catch his breath. They knew about his kiln? About the bodies down in the sublevels of his home? How had this Michael known they were down there, much less what he'd been about to do with them?

Moving to his office again, he sat down and looked at the two blood stains on the floor. The chair would need to be disposed of, as well as the carpet beneath it. He'd never purchased expensive things for this room for this very reason. He contemplated the conversation he'd just had with Michael, even though he tried his best to think he'd dreamed the entire thing up.

Judith was telling them things about him. The guy had to be a fed, just as Bonds had told him about. The problem was, he'd not been able to deal with the commissioner yet and the man could be telling them all sorts of things as well. Jerry tried to think what Bonds knew other than he was supposed to cover up the deaths of the three men at Jelly, Jams, and Preserves. A stupid name for a shop, but then she'd never had any business smarts.

Jerry sat there for another hour just telling himself, over and over, that things were not as bad as he thought, and that the conversation with Michael had never really happened and that he'd been overly tired. That was it. He was under a great deal of pressure and hadn't been sleeping well. Perhaps he needed to fly out west, get himself a hotel room and a couple of lovers, and forget about things for a while.

But this wasn't something he was going to let slow him, not when he was this close to the finish line. He just had to work faster, that was all. Pulling out his tablet, he began making corrections on his timeline.

Jerry had two shipments coming in the day after tomorrow, and then another one the next week. He wanted to have Judith with him during both these times because she'd be able to tell him when he was being watched. And she would, too, if she wanted to make it to her next birthday.

Jerry thought about what Michael had said about her. She was living with a man now, was she? That would help keep her in line if he were to get the guy and use him. Jerry would have to make use of this information, and nearly reached for the phone to tell Chad to get on it. But the blood stain was a reminder that he was no longer with him. As much as he hated to find another assistant, that was something else he was going to need to do and added it to his list under the heading, "Priority."

Finding Judith's man would be a piece of cake for him. It would be simple, he supposed, to call the man up, have him meet him for lunch, and take him then. Or he could go to her house, barge in, and take the man. Jerry wasn't stupid, he had been in this line of work for a long time, and taking one man would be easy enough with the right persuaders. A gun and rope would do the trick. Smiling, Jerry decided that first thing tomorrow he'd go to her house and wait for her to go out, then nab the man and bring him back here. Simple.

He was deep in his planning when he remembered the bodies in the basement. Jerry started to go down to start the cleaning up process when his phone rang. He answered it with a bark of his name and cringed when laughter greeted him.

"You should learn to be more polite when answering your device." Jerry snarled at the man, but he laughed harder. "I have called to tell you that you will not succeed in taking the man from her house. He is much smarter than you and a good deal stronger."

Jerry felt his entire mind seize up. Looking around the room, he tried to see where the cameras were hidden, and then looked down at his tablet. It had more information on it than any device he owned, and he wondered if the man who had sold it to him had lied about how safe it was. He'd purchased it because it was easy to destroy when necessary, but held all the information he needed at any given time.

"I have no cameras in your home, Jerrod Craft, nor do I have access to your little computer. I could, I suppose, but I do not." Jerry hadn't been called by his first name since…well, since his mother had died. "You should know that she is very disappointed in her sons. Very much so indeed. She said that her little donut would not have done so many bad things had she raised him better. I told her it wasn't her but you. You're simply a man who does not remember the upbringing she instilled within you."

Jerry put the phone in the cradle and then got up and unplugged it from the wall. He was suddenly very afraid. Not only did the man know about his plans, but Michael had as well. Someone was talking out of turn, and the sooner he found out who they were going to be dead. But it was far too late for him to stop now. It was far too late for a great many things.

Jerry was going to have to forget about the information that had come from the caller and the visit. First of all, he refused to believe it was real, and secondly…well, secondly he was going to kill whoever was telling on him. It would all fall to pieces before he could get Judith to him if he let a couple of crackpots fucking scare him off. Finishing his work, he found himself looking around the room more and more until he had to leave it. Setting up a temporary office in his dining room, he worked until he couldn't work anymore. It was well after midnight when he closed up his tablet, but he felt as if he'd made great progress. Things were going to go down in the morning.

He was in bed when he started to laugh. Judith was going to pay for giving him such a fright. There was no way that anyone but she knew about his mother and her calling him donut. It had been his passion as a child, eating donuts as if there would be no more of them. Judith had been very busy indeed if she knew that shit. She'd probably heard it from her father. And if he wasn't already dead, Jerry thought he'd find him and kill him again. Closing his eyes, he let sleep take him.

The dream settled over him slowly. The man he'd shared a cell with was sitting at a long table with someone Jerry had done a job with as a teenager. There were others there that he knew. Names not so much, but faces for sure. He found himself sitting at the head of the table when food was brought out to them on large platters. He could actually smell the roast beef and gravy. And he could almost swear that he could smell apple pie coming from somewhere deep within the house.

Conversations flowed easily enough around the table, he noticed. He caught up on information that was outdated but still fun to hear. His cell mate had told him a story about his first job, a story that Jerry had heard countless times before but still thought funny. He told it with such gusto that Jerry could swear that he'd been there with him.

Still food came to them. Platters of meat, steaming hot and rare looking, just the way he liked it. Bottles of wine were being poured into glasses around them, as well as potatoes and vegetables being served from wide bowls. Jerry never remembered eating any of the feast, but his plate was forever empty of anything but scraps of food and bits of gravy. Whenever he seemed to think about it, someone, a pretty man, would fill his plate again and he'd look at someone else to talk to.

The men who served them were also familiar. One he knew that he'd fucked for a month when he'd been let out of prison. Another had been someone he'd done as a kid. They didn't look any different to him, still young and beautiful. And some of them were actually naked. One such beauty offered his cock to him as he filled his plate. Jerry, of course, never one to turn down something free, suckled at him as he poured wine into the glasses he could reach easily. He thought about this cock being sucked by this man, and leaned back for him to take him when he moved away.

"You'll get your cock wet soon enough." He looked at the man who sat next to him. "They're all here for our pleasure, but not right now. We have things we must discuss before you are free to get your knob polished."

"Pleasure?" He nodded, and that's when Jerry realized who he was. "Lindale? What are you...? You're dead."

Lindale laughed and leaned back in his chair. "We all are. Not you, not yet at any rate, but we're all dead. By you."

"Me?" Jerry looked around the table and realized that his brother was correct. They were all dead, and now that he could see that, he noticed something else. Most of them were sporting the way they had been killed. Looking back at his brother, he could see the bullet hole in his forehead. He wanted to wake from this dream but was almost afraid not to hear what he had to tell him. The story of some Christmas show came to mind, and he laughed. But Lindale looked at him as if he knew what he'd been thinking.

"No one from your present or future is coming here to show you the errors of your ways. You were a great shot and that's all the nice things I'm going to say about you. As most of us can tell you." He laughed, and Jerry decided that he'd had enough of this dream and wanted to wake. "But we haven't even gotten to the good part yet. Do you not recognize the woman, too?"

"I don't want to." Lindale pulled one of the women to him and she sat on his lap. It took Jerry several minutes to release who she was. There was no mistaking his own wife. "She's dead. I know she is."

"You should, you moron, you killed me." He started shaking his head even as she stood up and showed him her neck. "Strangled me in my bath. What the hell, Jerry? I was good to you. I gave you whatever you wanted."

"You were fucking Lindale." The two of them looked at each other, and Jerry felt his body quake with anger. "You fucked him in our bed. In fact, you fucked him right before I killed you."

"His dick was so much bigger than yours. Wanna see it?" Before he could say no, Burl, his wife, dead these past seventeen years, knelt down in front of his dead brother and pulled out his cock. She was fisting him to hardness as Jerry felt his stomach twist up. When she took him into her mouth and gave him head, Jerry stood up. Before he could move out of this nightmare, he was pushed back down, and the young man from earlier was pulling Jerry's cock free.

The man had him in his mouth before he could push him away. He was sucking him like a vacuum, and Jerry closed his eyes to the nightmare around him as his cock was being polished. When he lifted the man's head to look at him, Jerry screamed. His lips were gone and one of his eyes had bugs falling from it. But it was the smile that had him screaming. Something that looked like meat was in his mouth, and Jerry looked down and saw that a large chunk of his cock was missing. The man spit it in his hand and handed it to him. Jerry started screaming immediately.

Jerry woke in his bed still screaming. Tearing from the bed, he went into the bathroom, stripped off his clothes, and stepped into the shower. He filled his sponge five times, scrubbing his cock as hard as he could every time. Then he poured the soap over his body and scrubbed it as well, the water as hot as he could make it until he was pink from it. When he got out, his cock was sore from all the scrubbing, as was his entire body.

As he was getting dressed, checking his dick every five minutes to make sure it was whole, something made him look at his bed. Jerry fell to the floor when he saw what was there, and threw up twice before he could make it to the bathroom. Two worms and a small bug were nestled in the middle of his bed, right where his ass would have been. Jerry knew he'd never sleep in that room ever again.

Chapter 6

Judith knew that Agon was close but not exactly where he was. She'd woken this morning to the phone ringing and had answered it without thinking. Starting her day off with speaking to her uncle had not been the highlight of her day. Now she was making blackberry preserves and things were not going well. The berries seemed to be turning to mush much faster than she'd expected.

"Of course it could be because I'm taking my aggressions out on them." She looked over at the bowl she'd been using and smiled. "Poor things. It's not their fault that my uncle is a fucking prick that thinks the world revolves around him."

Judith tossed the bowl of fruit across the room and watched it hit the wall. The art work it left behind made her laugh. She should have emptied it before getting that frustrated with it. But then, of course, she'd have no reminder of how shitty her morning was. And turning the berries into jelly instead of preserves wouldn't have been that difficult. She looked over at her monitor when someone knocked at the door. She should have known that Kala would be back.

Ignoring it wasn't an option. The woman was more determined to get in than Judith was to deny her entrance if her knocking was any indication. But when it stopped abruptly, she looked again. She was simply gone and Judith had a feeling it was not because she'd given up. Going to the door, she looked out the peep hole and tried to see her, but saw nothing but the back of her own home. Opening the door cautiously, she nearly screamed when Jerry was standing there. He was holding the woman with a gun to her head.

"Let her go and this will go much easier for you." He held a limp Kala in his arms, and Judith wondered if he'd harmed her children. "If you let her go, I'll come with you."

"You'll come with me all right. But she's my insurance." Judith crossed her arms over her chest and cocked a brow at him. She was terrified if she were truthful, not for herself but for the woman she'd come to like a little. "You think you can talk me out of taking this bitch with me, you're fucking insane."

"I don't even like her, so if you kill her then so be it." Judith tried to hide her fear from her uncle, but she wasn't sure it was working. "But if you don't let her go, you'll get shit from me even if you were to kill her." She started to close the door in his face, hoping to Christ she wasn't making the biggest mistake of her life when he spoke again.

"Then why do you care?" He put his gun to Kala's temple and held it there as he glared at her. Judith didn't move, not even to blink. She knew that it would be over if she did. Finally, Jerry tossed Kala at her, and she lowered her to the ground. Judith stood up and stepped around the fallen woman to move his attention from her. She'd made sure that the children were all right, and now she'd do what she should have done years ago. Fucking mess him up.

"I'm coming with you, but you should know it won't matter shit what you do to me. I'm not going to help you." He laughed, and she had to shake the fear that it gave her off her body. "You're going to pay for this. Maybe not today but soon. And when I have you where I want you, strapped to a chair with electricity going through your body, I'm going to dance a jig and get drunk afterwards."

"You think you can get one over me, Judith? I got news for you, I've been at this a good deal longer, and I'm pretty sure that you've never hurt anyone in your fucking life. But I'm going to...hurt you, I mean." He grabbed her arm and jerked her around so that she stumbled. When she was on her knees, she started to look up at him when something hit her from behind. Just as she was falling forward, she thought of Agon and wondered if he would come for her. But the ground smacked her in the face before she could think of why she wanted him to.

~~~

Judith opened her eyes and looked around the room. She didn't have any idea where she was, but she knew that she was alone. The chair she was tied to was the only piece of furniture in the room, and there was a single bulb hanging from a wire over her. She heard the door opening just as she realized there were no windows either. Jerry walked in holding his gun in front of him like a shield.

"So you finally woke up, did you?" Judith didn't answer him but smiled. "I'm guessing you think you can hold out on me. I'm thinking you don't have a chance when it comes to me getting what I want. I've perfected my ways of getting what I want from people. You'll be singing before long."

"I don't carry a tune all that well, but if you hum a few bars, maybe I can catch it." He looked at her like he had no idea what she was talking about. "Singing. You said I'd be singing. I was just...you know what? Never mind. Why am I here? I've told you countless times, I'm not going to help you. And where is here, by the way? Looks familiar but not—"

"You will. And as soon as I get that lover of yours, you'll give me what I want. He's very...large, isn't he?" Judith didn't say anything, knowing that if Jerry tangled with Agon, he'd be dead. "I'm going to bring him here and let you watch every time I slice into him when you don't answer me. I think it will be good for both of us. You'll get to see that I fucking mean business, and I'll get to kill someone that you love. A win-win situation for me and a...well, not so much for you."

"Good luck on that shit." He reached behind him in the hall and pulled a chair into the room. He had a file with him and a small tablet, but it was the chair that had her full attention. She knew it. It had been a very long time, but she knew where he'd gotten it and had a pretty good idea where they were. "We're at my dad's old house. Well, if that don't make the monkey shit in the corner and say fuck me." He looked at her oddly, then shook his head.

"Very good. You should also know that someone has been keeping it up for me. The place doesn't look like anyone has moved even a stick of furniture since the night I killed off your daddy. I will have to thank them. It's even been dusted." She started to tell him she didn't want his thanks but only sat there. "Did you know that this house and all its contents were supposed to come to me when he died? As your only living relative, this should have come to me, not you. I was wondering about who got it when you sent me off to prison, and went to downtown to see who would be morbid enough to do that. And you know what I discovered? That no one knows who owns this place. They have a record of the taxes being paid, in cash I might add, but they cannot find a name of the owners. Do you happen to know who that might be?"

She knew they would never find the name. She'd worked very hard in keeping that quiet. And the man she had helping her would never say a word either. He would just shuffle the files around and simply ignore any requests to find out. As long as the taxes were paid up, he told her she'd be safe. Paul Whittaker was a good friend.

Jerry was looking over the tablet when she thought of Kala. She didn't have to ask him but simply closed her eyes. She was relieved to see that not only was she safe in her husband's arms, but she was spitting mad as well. When she looked into her eyes to see if she was all right, she saw Agon there and her heart ached to touch him.

"I have two deals going down tonight and I want you to tell me if I can go there to get the shit myself, or should I send in a dummy to get it for me?" When she didn't answer him, he looked at her. "I've not hurt you yet, but if you don't answer me, I certainly will."

"I'm just trying to figure out who else you consider a dummy besides you. I mean, you're the dumbest person I know if you think I'm going to give you any information. And what if I'm lying to you? Have you thought of that?"

When he stood up, Judith braced herself for the hit. As soon as his fist slammed against her mouth and her head jerked around from the impact, she laughed. She hurt, there was no way that she wouldn't have, but she didn't care so long as he didn't get what he wanted. Spitting the blood from her mouth onto the floor, she just stared at him.

"You're going to do as I say or so help me I'll...I'll...." Judith laughed again. "You fucking bitch, this is not funny."

"Of course it is. You want something from me, yet you think that just because you're not tied to a chair and I am, that I should give it to you. I find that to be extremely funny." She watched him draw back again and she lifted her chin. "You can hit me until you hurt, but you'll get nothing."

The third or maybe the fourth time he hit her, she felt herself slipping away. Pain radiated from her head in ways that had her thinking she'd have no teeth left, not to mention not a single rib in her body wouldn't be broken when this was over. She surrendered to the pain and let it pull her away from it.

~~~

Agon paced the room several times before he sat down. He wanted to go and find her, but no one would help him. Looking at Kala, he felt his heart twist just a little more. She could have been killed and no one had been there to protect her. Neither of them.

"I'm fine. He just surprised me is all." Riss didn't let go of her hand but smoothed her forehead again as Kala continued. "I was trying to get Judith to come to the door and suddenly I was out. I'm pretty sure he hit me with a gun."

"You are not helping, love." She looked over at him when Riss spoke. "He has been forbidden to go after her. And he is not...let me just say he is not a happy person. I

96

have been trying to go to Boss on his behalf, but He will not listen to me either.

"You love her?" Agon nodded at her question. "I'm assuming you haven't told her yet then. That would be one reason why you're here and she's not. Why does it take you men forever to tell someone that you have feelings for them? Are you afraid that we'll want something more? Or are you just stupid?"

"I have not told her, no. I only just discovered this last evening before I was summoned away." Agon got up to pace again and ended up at the window to the backyard. "She will not be happy with my declaration, I think. But as much as I did not want her in my life, I want her there now more than I've ever thought possible. How was I to know that this would be the best thing that has ever happened to me?"

"You should have told her. And we tried to tell you. But being the stubborn jackass that you are, you didn't listen, did you?" He nodded at Kala without turning around. "What do you know about the man who took her? I mean, do you have a name at least? Or a description of him?"

"Her uncle, Jerry Craft. He wishes to use her abilities to gain more than he needs. I do believe that he will kill her when he has no more use of her." Agon heard Kala snort and smiled. "She will not give him anything, and I fear...no not fear, but I almost feel sorry for the man. He will understand stubbornness like he has never known." Agon smiled, thinking of how stubborn she really was. "Do you think it would be rude of me to request to find her so that I may watch her make this man mad? It would be a show worth watching, I believe." Everyone laughed, and Agon felt a little better for it.

"She is a little on the stubborn side. Did you know that she has a great deal of money in the bank?" Agon looked at Kala when she spoke. "She has just over ninety million dollars from investments she's made with the money her father gave her through insurance. She wasn't going to take it at first, but then about a month after she turned eighteen, she had the bank set her up with a trading account and she started making money hand over fist. Then there is the money that he left her in cash. From what my investigator can find, she's never touched a dime of that either. But she does donate a great deal of her millions to other causes. Her favorite place to make a difference is at the local schools. She donates enough money to run them for the first three months of the session."

"She will think it bad money." He turned and walked back to the chair he'd been out of more than in and sat down. "I should like to know what else you have found out. If I am to marry her, then having information would be helpful."

"I don't know why. She knows nothing of you, yet you love her." Agon nodded. "Tell me something, do you know why you weren't with her when this happened? Do you think it was some grand plan that you were away when she needed you most?"

"I do. But I am not going to question Him. I'm beginning to think that the more I ask Him, the harder He makes it on me." Agon leaned back in his chair. "I think she must want me to come to her. I am not sure how that would work, as she is, as we've pointed out, very stubborn. But Judith will need to...she will need to need me, I think."

"And how is it that you're supposed to know that she needs you if you don't know where she is?" He didn't have an answer, but it mattered little to Kala. She was on a roll, as Riss was forever saying, and she would not be dissuaded from her thought process. "I want you to think about the places you've seen her at. I mean really think."

He closed his eyes and thought of every time he'd seen her. The building she worked in, the house where she lived. He thought of the gardens behind her house that strung along the building like rows of little soldiers on patrol. Agon even thought of the images that Boss had shown him, the way she'd been sitting on a porch swing with the breeze blowing her long locks into her face. There was a number there, and he paused in his need to look at her to see the numbers on the house. Then he saw the mail laying in her lap.

"Her childhood home is nearby here. She has not been there in a good many years I think. Not since her father was killed. There is a swing on the front stoop that was green and yellow; planters on the hanger behind her but the flowers are long since dead." He focused on the mail and tried to read what it said. "Humble Street. Her family home was on Humble Street."

"I know where that is." Agon stood up and looked at Riss when he started for the door. "We can go over there and see if there are any clues."

"I will go." Riss started to argue, but Kala cleared her throat. One look at her and Riss nodded at him. "I will see what I can find out ab—"

Agon?

He stood there for several seconds, a pain radiating from his mind to his heart. It had come onto him so suddenly that it had taken his breath away. Agon could hear Riss saying his name, but the pain was almost too much. When he looked again, Boss was lowering him to the floor gently.

"She has called for us." Agon nodded and started to stand. "We will leave directly. You must rest a moment."

"I need to go to her." Boss nodded but wouldn't let him stand. "She needs me. I need to make sure she is well."

"As we will, but first you must allow me to go to her." Agon started to tell Him no, but Boss spoke again. "She and I have to...she will need Me first."

"She is hurt." Boss nodded. "Badly? If so, then You must save her. I will not...I cannot live without her, my Lord. Please, you must."

"I will do what she will allow Me to do. I will call for you when I am ready." He disappeared before Agon could ask Him to hurry.

Agon stared at Galin when he appeared. "You are to help me?" Galin grinned, but shook his head. "You are to hold me here then. I will not allow you to do so, my brother. I need my love."

"And I'm pretty sure in your current condition that you will not get past me." Galin grinned wider. "Of course, if you promise me that should you hear of me getting a wife you tell me straight away, then I might be happy to allow you to hit me. Once. It would not be good for you to simply get by me."

"You'd let me hit you?" Galin nodded and put out his chin. "Then I would gladly concede to your wishes."

Agon knew enough about fighting to know that to hit someone in the chin like Galin was offering him would hurt them both. The face had a great many bones in it and its purpose was to protect the head, not to give easily. So instead of hitting him with his fist, Agon let go some of his power and tossed Galin across the room, where he hit the wall. He was struggling to get up when Agon stood. He was gone before Galin could regain his feet.

The house was quiet, but he could hear sounds. Some of them were animals beyond the house, other noises were sounds of the house itself, creaking and groaning sounds that only an older house would have. He entered the front door quietly and found that he was in the room from the memory that Boss had shown him. The cage was still sitting in the corner where she'd been held.

The house didn't smell of anything that would tell him she was there. He could smell the faint smell of cleaner as well as a lemony polish that one of Jerry's charges had used weekly on the piano no one played. He moved to the small table that sat in front of the couch and could see a cup of something steaming there. Leaning to it, he could smell the strong coffee as the scent ascended from it. Someone else was there, and he knew it wasn't Judith. She did not drink this beverage.

Moving toward the other room, Agon stopped and looked back. Something was incorrect about the room. It took him a few seconds to realize that there was a chair missing, and it had been dragged out of this room toward the one he was headed to. Going into what happened to be the kitchen, he wasn't surprised to find this room, like the one beyond, was cleaned as well. He moved toward the three doors in the room.

The first one was to a pantry. He left the door ajar once he saw that no one hid in it. There were no foodstuffs within either, so he decided that if someone lived there, they did not stock the large room. The second door, the one that had a window boarded over, led to the backyard.

Looking at the floor when he heard an odd sound, he noticed the glass. Someone had broken into this house and had tried to cover their tracks by covering the broken window. Agon moved to the third and final door.

The handle turned easily enough, but he still did not open the door, moving through it in favor of not alerting the person below. If there was someone there, he'd use his powers to help Judith and to keep himself safe as well. He nearly went to her when he saw the woman there.

"You should not have come." He looked over at Boss as He stared at the woman. "She is in grave shape, but she has asked that I not take her as yet."

"Take her?" He looked at the woman and only then realized it was Judith. "She is going to die?"

"She will if nothing is done soon." Agon started for her but stopped when Boss put His hand on his chest. "Judith needs this as much as you do. Please do not let her last wish be for naught."

"I love her. I do not...please do not allow her to die. I have...please." Agon dropped to his knees and then lower, spreading his wings out in a way that showed all that he was. "I beg of you, my Lord. Do not allow her to die. Take me instead."

"I can only do what she has asked of Me, Agon. Her wish, like yours, was to save you at all costs. She has begged Me for this." Agon looked up at Boss as he wiped away a tear. "You must allow this to happen so that she will come to Me."

Agon was lifted up and held to watch as a man entered the room. He did not see them, of course, but he moved to Judith. He had a gun in his hand and before Agon could have stopped him, he shot Judith in the leg.

Blood poured from her wound and yet she did nothing but lift her head.

"You're going to pay for this." Jerry laughed and lifted the gun again. But before he could do anything at all, a sound from the upper levels made him pause. "See, I told you you'd pay."

He shot her again, this time in the chest. As he fled, going toward an opening at the rear of the room, Jerry was cursing loudly. As soon as Boss let him go, Agon went to her side and put his hand over the wound in her chest. She looked at him for several seconds before she smiled.

"I thought of you, and here you are." He nodded, his heart heavy with her pain. "I never knew that trusting someone could be so painful. But then I guess love hurts."

"You love me?" Her head rolled to the side just as two men came down the stairs with their guns drawn. Even as one of them checked her pulse, the other was calling for an ambulance. "I will not leave you."

"I think I might like that. But you're not sleeping with me again." He burst out laughing at her tone and watched as she was cut loose from the chair. The officer that was lowering her to the floor told her he couldn't sleep with her right now, but maybe later.

"He means to comfort her." Agon looked at Conley, another protector. He was watching the officer. "My charge has been hurt before and knows that sometimes things are said that mean nothing. He does not know she speaks to you."

"She is going to be my wife." Conley nodded but said nothing as his charge covered Judith with his coat. She was shaking now but he kept talking to her. When Agon turned to speak to Boss, he realized He'd left him. He stayed, holding her hand even when the medics came.

"She has lost a lot of blood," Agon heard one of the men say. Others talked about her wounds and how close they were to her heart. Then another said that she was weak, and that if she made it to surgery, it would be a miracle. Agon said nothing to these men, but did to their protectors.

"Tell them to be more positive when speaking. She can hear them." The newest protector nodded but stood doing nothing. "You heard me, I said to give her encouragement, not tell her she is to die."

"But she is to die." Agon had to take several breaths when the man shook his head. "You should know that as well as we do. She had nothing going for her."

Agon called for Riss, and he was there in seconds with another man, another protector. The first man disappeared when Riss did, and the new man was talking to the medic and telling him what to say.

"She has a fighting chance. Her body is strong and her heart rate not critical." They all knew that it was. Even the protector knew it for the lie that it was, but no one was talking negatively to her any longer.

The ride to the hospital was the longest of his life. Agon moved into the operating room when she did and watched as the men and women there scrambled to help his one true love. They worked hard to bring her back to him. Her heart stopped twice, and both times Boss appeared to whisper in her ear. Agon watched as they retrieved two spent bullets, shot from the gun that her uncle had used. The sound of them hitting the small silver pans echoed loudly in the still room. Still he never left her, not even when he was summoned by Michael.

"You should come to me when I call." Agon didn't acknowledge the man who he had known all his life. "I have something I need you to do."

"I'll not leave her." Michael stood in front of him, and Agon looked down at him. "You will try to make me and may succeed, but I will not leave willingly. Not ever again."

Michael stared at him for several seconds before nodding. As soon as the surgeon said that he was finished, Agon moved closer to the bed and took her hand into his again. Kissing it gently on the back, he leaned to her mouth and gave her as much of himself as he could in the form of his breath. He waited. In seconds her heart skipped several beats before it picked up a little better. As she was moved to another room, Agon reached for Riss again.

I will need you to do some things for her. I believe I have defied Michael and Boss one too many times and when this is over, I believe they will punish me in ways that I would not like to think about too hard. Riss said nothing, but Agon knew the consequences for saving a life that was not his to save. *I should like for you to keep her safe, please. I have monies that I'd like for you to —*

No. I will not. You will have to deal with this…what were you thinking stepping in like this? Boss is livid, and He said you must be punished severely. I have never seen Him so angry in all my lifetime. Agon knew that his friend would do whatever Boss told him, and he did not blame him at all for being upset with him as well. *You will go to Him. Now, Agon. He will speak to you now. I will watch over Judith for you, but He wishes you to come now. I would do so now before whatever He has planned for you comes before He can speak.*

Agon said he'd go now, and he waited only long enough for Riss to come to him so that he could watch

Judith. As soon as he appeared, Agon hugged his friend tightly to him and told him how much he loved him. Before he left him, knowing it would more than likely be the last time he saw him, Agon hugged him again and disappeared.

Chapter 7

Boss watched the man pace. He wanted to go and hug him, but was fearful that all would be lost if He did. Things were going to have to go the way they were set or Judith would still die. He was both in awe of Agon for his bravery and upset that the man had done what he'd done. Few, very few, would live after defying Him.

When he was showed into the room with Him, Michael sat down across from Him. Agon stood near the door and gripped whatever it was he had in his hand. Boss knew, of course, and again was proud of him. When He motioned for him to have a seat, Agon nodded but only moved to stand near His desk.

"I have brought You my things. All that was given to me when I was created." The packet was laid on the desk, but He did not touch it. "I've shamed myself as much as I have You, and I know that things will…I only ask that You know I acted on my own. No one helped me in any way with my decision in the course of actions that—"

"Riss says that he told you to go to Judith. Conley said that he allowed you to hit him so that you could go to her as well. Kala has informed me that she told you where to go and that she drove you to the house to defy Me. All these people tell Me that they acted alone and that you were only doing what they bid because you feared for them. They, too, have offered Me their things in the hopes that I'd punish them instead of you."

"I do not know what to say about that. They did not help me in any way. This I swear to You. I did not fear for anyone but the woman that I love." Agon stood up straighter and pointed to the thing on the desk. "I would ask that You not make anyone suffer for what I did. No one helped me in any way, no one allowed me anything but told me to stay where You had told me and to heed Your words."

"Yet you did not." Agon nodded and dropped to his knees again. "You would ask Me forgiveness now, Agon? After the fact that had you not stepped in where you were expressly told not to go, that Judith would be dead now?"

"I do not ask You for forgiveness, my Lord. I know that it would not be given, and I do not wish to plead for my life but that of Judith." Boss leaned back in His chair as Agon continued. "I should like for her to be given the chance to live a full and happy life. I have…you know that I have given her a part of me so she will not die, but I would ask that she help with the training of others like Riss. She has a good heart and a wonderful mind. I believe she will be a good addition to his team."

"So you think that because you saved her, you should be responsible for her life now?" Agon shook his head and pointed to the packet on his desk again. Boss picked it up and dumped the contents on the table. What was in it surprised even Him. "You wish for her to have this?"

"Yes. I wish for her to have all that I am. And I do feel responsible for her, and no matter when my death comes, I will continue to do so then too. She is…she will forever be my wife; if not in life, then in my heart for sure." Boss picked up the medallion and held it up by the chain. The glimmering gold reflected off the walls, and Boss put it back on the desk as He ran His fingers over it. The change was immediate and He smiled.

"You will convince her to marry you posthaste." Agon looked at Him with a confused look. "If she does not agree, and I mean immediately, then you and I will continue to have this conversation, but the outcome will not be a good one. She will be your wife today or there will be no hope for you."

"But she is…what I mean to say, my Lord, how will I do that when she is still recovering from her surgery?" Agon looked at Michael when He didn't say anything. "She was near death when I left her. I cannot see how she will be agreeing to anything when she is not in a state of mind to agree or disagree with me."

"I have…she is in the hallway. Not her but her spirit. And just so that you know, her spirit is just as stubborn as she is." Agon stood up and then dropped again. Boss let him go with a wave, and he moved out of the room.

Boss sat there for several seconds before He looked at Michael. "You are very sly, My good man. How did you do this without My knowledge?" Michael laughed, and Boss lifted His brow. "You will tell Me or I shall simply look."

"I have a trick or two up my sleeve as well. You were surprised, were you not, that he would give over something that would end his life so horribly? The risk of giving you his soul back in the form of the medallion would have cost us all dearly. I did not…I knew that he loved her, but not to what extent." Boss looked at the new crest that was Agon's to have. "The other world would have welcomed him."

"But he was never theirs to take, and now he will marry or I will have to think of something cleverer to blackmail him with." Michael nodded, and they both turned to the door when a loud voice penetrated the thick wood. "However, after this, he may ask Me to send him on his way rather than face her again. She is...how is it they say? Pig-stronged?"

"I believe it is pig-headed. And she is that and more." Another noise had them both standing, but neither of them moved to see what was going on. "She will make him happy once he convinces her that she is going to be so."

"I do believe you are correct. And in the meantime, it will be fun to watch them get to the point." Boss looked down at the medallion again. "She will need to be marked soon. I do not wish to see her in such a state again. See to it as soon as possible."

Michael nodded and left Him. Boss knew that it would be a few hours before Agon came to Him again. He looked at the pictures on the wall that served as his wallpaper. He had been looking at these men and women for nearly a thousand years, waiting for the other halves to be born. He glanced at Galin's picture and wondered what the man would think when he found his own wife was so close. Sadly, he opened his computer and started to work, knowing that whatever he thought, it was as good as done. And as soon as things progressed with Galin's wife to be, He'd have to work twice as hard to help her. Things were about to heat up for the girl and her nephew.

~~~

"I will not be blackmailed." Judith paced the large room and tried to think what she was doing there and not...well, dead. She knew that Jerry had shot her several times and had stabbed her even more. By all accounts she should be dead. But the man sitting on the oversized bed only had one thought in his head, and that was for her to marry him.

"I would hope that you would come into this easily." She stopped her pacing to stare at him when he spoke. "There is much to be said for marriage. And we will have a long and very productive one."

"You think...productive? How the hell...productive? Are you planning to put me to work as soon as the 'I dos' are said?" He looked at her as if he had no idea what she was talking about, but she knew that he did. Just knew it. "I suppose you want me to do the things I wouldn't do for my uncle. Well, it's not going to happen, buddy. I'm not going to help you get rich with my horrors."

"I do not need your money. I have...we have plenty of our own. Not counting yours, Riss tells me that we will never have to spend anything but the interest to live very nicely." Agon frowned as he stood up. "I do not know what my interest in the money has to do with us living, but he assured me that there is more than enough to go around."

"He doesn't mean your interest, but the money you can earn by having your money in a bank." Judith shook her head. "You're distracting me again. I was telling you that Boss or whatever it is you call Him will just have to get over it. There is no reason whatsoever for me to marry you. I'm perfectly happy to be alone."

"Yet you called for me." Judith backed away from Agon when he started for her. "You called for me and I knew to come to you. It was that and your love for me that saved you."

"I don't love you. I like you well enough, but I don't love you." He was close enough for her to touch him, yet she put her hands behind her back. "Why are you forever standing practically on top of me?"

"Because I would like nothing more than to be inside of you." He touched his mouth to her shoulder, and she closed her eyes. "I was not aware that in this form I could touch you. Do you have any idea what your skin tastes like to me? How your scent seemingly was made for me and only me?"

"What do you mean 'in this form'?" His mouth moved over her shoulder to her throat and she tilted her head back so he could nip at her skin. "Answer me, please?"

"You are a spirit here in this place. Your body is recuperating at the hospital after the surgery. Will you let me taste your mouth again, Judith?" She nodded, and his mouth made its way to just below her ear, then to her mouth. He drew her lower lip into his mouth as she reached for and held onto the dresser behind her. "You are so warm and inviting."

"Agon, you're not going to make love to me. I don't want you to." She knew he had figured out she was lying when he chuckled. Before she could pull him from her body, if she ever wanted to, he ran his tongue over her lips. "Agon, you're not playing fair."

"And I have no wish to play at all unless it is with your body." He took her mouth again, this time devouring her as he lifted her up and sat her on the dresser she had been using as a post. Wrapping her legs around him, she tore at his clothing to simply touch him. When his chest was bared to her, she pushed him back enough that she could take his nipple into her mouth and suckle it. His fingers curled into her hair and instead of pulling her away, he pressed her harder to him.

When he did lift her head up, she looked into his eyes and saw that he did truly love her. As much as she knew that love was not real, she knew that he would show her things that no one had ever shown her before. Happiness for one thing, unconditional love for the second.

"You love me." He nodded and pulled her mouth to his for a gentle kiss. "I don't know how to love you, Agon. I have never loved anyone before."

"I would love to show you. I will…I cannot help but to love you no matter what." He picked her up again, this time cradled in his arms. "I would very much like to make love to you now. To be buried deep within you would be something we can both enjoy."

She knew he was right and let him lay her on the bed. They'd had sex before, not a great deal of it but enough that she knew that he was inexperienced in it. But she knew that this time would be different, this time he would not just tell her he loved her, but he would show her as well. As he stood over her staring down at her, she felt her body flush with need. His smile told her he knew it too.

"Take off your clothes." He stood there looking at her when she repeated herself. "I want to see you, all of you."

"You will return the favor?" She nodded as he pulled his shirt over his head. "There are ways for me to be naked without this removing of clothing one piece at a time. And I can do the same to you. But I want to see you take them off for me, take each garment off and drop it to the floor like this."

His shirt slipped from his fingers as the silken material seemed to glide to the floor. Judith watched as he removed his belt slowly and it, too, joined the shirt. By the time he had his pants off and he stood only in his silk boxers, she was panting to see all of him. As he backed up and helped her to stand beside him, he started unbuttoning the blouse she'd had on earlier today. He was taking his time with it, and she found that it was the sexiest thing that anyone had ever done to her.

"I guess being here takes away the horror of when I was taken." He nodded and kissed her neck. The blouse added to the pile on the floor as she kicked off her shoes and pulled off her pants, leaving her panties on with her bra. "I have never undressed like this before. I have been naked during sex, but I never...I never undressed before."

"You will please me greatly if you do not speak of other bed partners." He kissed her neck again. "I will stop now, but it is hard for me not to want to taste you thusly."

"You want to eat me again?" He nodded, and she slid her hand down his chest to his cock. "You can if you want, but I want to take you into my mouth at the same time. Would you like that?"

"How is this possible?" She could see the need on his face, and he lay on the bed as she instructed. "Come to me, Judith. I wish to be inside of you now."

"Not yet. I have plans for your body, and I find that I don't want to hurry through it just now." When she went to the other side of the bed, he started to turn. "No, stay this way. I'm going to show you something."

As soon as she crawled down his body, he starting kissing her, touching her. By the time she got to his silk-covered cock she was almost too needy to do more than swallow him down and have him take her. Rubbing her cheek over his cock, she felt him rock his hips upward and she nipped at his shaft.

Before she could tell him what she wanted him to do, he pulled her down over his mouth and ate at her through her panties. Judith cried out and rolled her hips downward for him to take her again and again. She couldn't believe how good he was at this and felt her body expand and heat just for him. Judith looked down at his cock again and wanted to taste him. She wanted him to slide down her throat, too, as he came in her mouth. She pulled his briefs down and licked the crown of his cock.

His cock was so thick and hard that she had to fight with his boxers to free him. By the time she had him freed, she was so close to coming all over his mouth that she had to take several deep breaths to slow things down. As soon as she wrapped her mouth around his crown again, Agon nipped at her clit and she screamed out her release. He continued to eat her, lapping at her over-sensitive flesh until she was peaking again.

His cock was streaming precum like he had already come. She licked him over and over to take him into her body before swallowing him down. He surged up so hard that she gagged slightly, but he was fucking her mouth, and she wanted to feel him come this way. Concentrating on him and not what he was doing to her pussy, she cupped his balls in her hand and rolled them. He let her pussy go with a roar as he filled her mouth and throat with his cum.

Judith wanted to make him come again, but he rolled her to her back and stood up. She nearly got up as well when he fisted his cock using her saliva and his cum to make himself hard again. Licking her lips, she could taste him there and slid her hand down to her pussy to let him see how ready she was for his cock.

"You would come this way, would you not?" She nodded and moaned when her finger brushed over her nubbin. "Tasting you has only whetted my appetite for more of you. My cock, I would very much like to bury myself into you."

Spreading her legs, she entered her pussy with two of her fingers. She watched as he moved up and down his cock over and over. Sitting up, she rolled to her knees and told him to come to her.

"Fuck me this way." He moved up behind her and she felt his cock at her entrance. "Fuck me, Agon. Use your strength to take me to the bed and fuck me."

He didn't need any more instructions and slammed his cock deep inside of her. As he powered into her, she slid her fingers over her clit again until he joined her with his fingers as well. She was wet enough that he could slide his fingers into her sheath as he took her. When he bit into her shoulder, something that she'd never enjoyed before, Judith screamed out his name and came so hard that darkness took her. Her last thoughts were that he'd killed her, and she smiled.

When she opened her eyes, he was holding her. She heard his soft breathing and knew that he slept as well. Getting up as quietly as she could, she dressed in a pair of his boxers she'd pulled from his dresser and found one of his silk shirts in his closet. As she moved out of his room and down the hall, she couldn't help but smile.

Finding the office she wanted wasn't as hard as she thought it would be. After knocking once she was told to enter, and she looked at the man sitting behind the desk.

Without being asked, she sat down in the chair and looked at Him.

"You will need to return soon." She nodded but didn't move. Boss leaned back from His keyboard and regarded her. "Have you come to tell me you have decided to marry our Agon?"

"I have a few questions first." She looked around the room, then back at Him. "You planned this entire thing, didn't You?"

"I planned two things, but am glad you have chosen this one." Judith nodded, and He continued. "You have queries, as do I. May we trade them, you one, then Me one?"

"Okay. But I'll tell you what I tell anyone who wants to ask me questions. I'm not going to sugarcoat the answers. Especially when I'm pretty sure You already know the answers."

"I do." He smiled as He continued. "But I would still like to hear what you have to say. Especially since we both know you have free will. My first question is this; your uncle, you had the means to have him put to death, yet you did not. Why?"

"I'm not going to...why didn't You?" He shrugged. "I didn't have him put to death because it was always my hope that he would come to love me. As you can see, that failed big time."

"Failed? I suppose in a way that it did. But not for you. How would you have felt if you had done it back then?" She thought about it but didn't say anything. What would be the point? "Judith, you must answer the questions."

"I would have always wondered." She got up to pace and wandered over to a window that looked out over a lovely field of tulips. "My father wasn't a good man. My uncle...well, you know what he is, too. But what of my mother? No one has ever told me a thing about her. I asked, but after a while gave up on that, too."

"She was a wonderfully amazing woman. You're a great deal like her, as a matter of fact. Just before she slipped into her death, she called to Me to save you. Not herself, mind you, but you. I came to see you immediately." She turned to look at Him. "Yes, you were still in her womb, as you know, but you were still her child and I would do most anything for her."

"I heard once, a very long time ago, that she was always doing things for others. It was at the trial of my uncle. There was word that...." She looked at Boss. "Did he kill her? Either of them, did they kill her?"

She didn't think He was going to answer her. When He asked her to sit, she started to tell Him never mind, she really didn't want to know, but she did move toward the chair. When she was seated, He waved His hands at the wall and a picture appeared. It was her mother. She had no idea why she knew that, but there she was.

"This was right before the accident. She and your father were getting into the car, but he told her he had other arrangements and left her." The picture started to move like a movie, and she watched as her mother got into the car alone and rubbed her belly. She leaned down and started telling her baby how much she loved her. "Your mother wanted you a great deal. Loved you more than anything in this world. It was why I went to you."

As the movie moved forward, she watched as her mother drove cautiously and with care, stopping at the two stop signs and looking both ways before moving forward. The sudden shift in the car had the view turning to look behind them at the next stop sign as a large SUV rammed her a second then a third time. The fourth time it hit them, everything went blurry for several seconds. The next part of the movie was of her mother in a hospital bed with her head bandaged up and wires running from every part of her.

"He shoved her into traffic." Boss nodded. "Why? What did she do to him that he'd have to kill her for?"

"Your father thought that you were your uncle's child." Judith stared at Boss as He continued. "It wasn't true, of course. She'd never do such a thing, but he thought it. The only reason you were saved is because the protector that was with your father was able to convince him that killing you would serve no purpose, and if you lived it would guarantee more sympathy for him when you were born. Your father was nothing if not vain."

"Who?" She wanted to know the protector's name and was sure He wasn't going to give it to her, so she asked Him again. "Who do I owe my life to? I need to...I know him, don't I? I know the man who saved my life."

"You do. He is Galin." He handed her a picture of the man who had saved her, and she committed it to memory. This man would have whatever he wanted from her forever. "He will not appreciate you knowing. I believe he is...well, he is sad for you. Not that you have lived, but because you have suffered so much for what he did."

"He saved me." Boss shrugged. "He gave me what no one has given me since. A chance. I owe him my life."

"He will only see that he put you in harm's way." She looked at the movie where her mother was still in the hospital. She was so beautiful even in all her pain.

Looking at Boss, she asked Him what had been on her mind since she woke. "Will I be an immortal like Agon?

Will I be able to go up against Jerry and defeat him if I'm not?" He nodded and smiled at her. "This body that I'm in now, it's not…it's not real, is it?"

"Nay, it is not. You are whole here, as you know, but you are not the woman who hangs onto life so tightly in the hospital. The life that you have here is only possible because when you lay injured, Agon gave you a piece of him, a breath from his body into yours. Now you will heal much faster. You'll wake in a few hours, back in your body with these memories and a body that will live for as long as you wish. Forever, if that is your desire." He stood up, and she did as well. "Agon is searching for you. He has it in his head that I have spirited you away and sent you home again."

As she made her way to the door with Him behind her, she turned and looked at Him. There was something there, a spark of something she had long forgotten. And when she remembered it fully, she smiled at Him. He smiled back.

"You told me once that I would need you, and that only then would I come to you willingly." He nodded, and His smile broadened. "I need you."

With that she turned and walked from the room and down the hall. She met Agon just as he was coming out of a room. He picked her up and hugged her tightly to him, and she felt all was right with the world. Kissing him gently on the mouth, she looked up at him.

"I'm in love with you. And if you still want to, I'll marry you." The sound of his happiness bounced from wall to wall until several others came out of their rooms and stared at them. He told each and every one of them that he had a wife and that she loved him. Judith knew that for as long as she lived, she'd never be as happy as she was right then.

Chapter 8

Jerry wanted to get out of his room but was terrified that someone would recognize him. His picture had been plastered all over the media since he'd fled the house two days ago. And now it seemed that someone — and he knew just who the *someone* was — had told all they knew about the bodies on his land. As soon as he found her, Judith was going to be dead.

"The excavation of the property began late last night when authorities were given a tip on the smell coming from the house."

That was another thing that he was pissed about. How the hell did anyone smell anything coming from his house? He was four miles from the road and his closest neighbor was more than ten football fields away. But the news reporter went on about the bodies in the basement and her opinion on why they were where they were.

"The kiln — a furnace or oven, you may know, used for baking pottery, grain, or bricks — was stuffed with the body of one Janice Holloway, known to her friends as Jane. The police

aren't saying much right now, but it looks as if she might be involved in foul play. The man with her, his identity unknown at this time, was also in the basement, but near the kiln and not actually inside of it. It is thought that he might have been next in the ghastly firing. We are still waiting on details as to what the police think might have transpired."

"What transpired, you moron, was I forgot to turn the kiln on so that there would be no evidence of anything. Mother fuck." He glared at the television more as the woman droned on and on about what was suspected. "All I had to do was go down there and turn it on. I could have even put the chair and rug in there too and been done with the whole thing. But oh no, I had to answer the door and now look at this shit."

Jerry got up to go to the bathroom to see his face. When he'd been running out of the house he'd cut his cheek badly. He knew that it needed stitches, but right now he was too hot to go and find himself a good doctor to sew it up. And the worst part was, he'd left his DNA all over the fucking house where Judith was. Jerry carefully pulled the gauze off and looked at the long gash.

It was perhaps four inches long, from his nose to just below his ear. And deep. He could have sworn at first he could see his teeth and gums through it, but it was just raw muscle. And the swelling was bad, too. Every time he tried to chew, it hurt him so badly that he wanted to sob. He was going to kill the fucking bitch if she didn't die from his beatings. And from all accounts, she wasn't going to, either.

The paper said she'd been in critical condition when he'd first heard about her. Then an hour later, she was upgraded to guarded. Today, not forty-eight hours later, she was being released. What the fuck was that all about? He wondered.

"And here I am, a pillar of the community, suffering all kinds of pain, and she's being treated like a queen. The fucking cunt should have never been born." Jerry sat back down on the bed and glared at the now muted television. He was frankly sick to death of hearing about each little thing they came across at his home, too. What were they thinking a man like him would have? Flowers and tea parties? Or were they thinking he'd been running a half-way house for degenerates or something?

"I'm a fucking thief and murderer." He moaned at the pain when he screamed at the television again and laid back. "This fucking sucks. I need my house. There are things there that they'll never find, and I want them."

Like his passports and money. He could go anywhere he wanted with the seven or eight false identifications he'd made long ago. There was the safe, too, the one he'd bought the house for. It was hidden so deeply in the basement that not even a metal detector could find it. Laughing to himself, he looked at the television again. He reached for the remote when he saw Judith.

"...to the house in a good many years. I think that when I was a child I might have been here, but there has been so much tragedy in my life that I could be mistaken." Her face was badly bruised still, and that made him smile, but she continued before he could do more than gloat a little. "I know that at one time there was a large vault in the sub levels. I'm going in now to help the investigators find it."

Jerry screamed at the camera again and again as it followed Judith into the house. She was followed by a large man, and Jerry knew that he was the man who was going to marry the bitch. Standing up, he decided that laying there wasn't getting him anything. It was time to go out and get his revenge.

It took him over an hour to find a taxi company willing to take him out there, and then a forty-minute drive in the smelliest vehicle he'd ever been in. By the time he was let off in front of the drive a block from his home, he was sure he reeked of the dirt in the back of the thing. Jerry walked down the street bemoaning what had befallen him.

"I just wanted to help her make ends meet. Why am I the bad guy in all this?" He laughed at himself. Making ends meet had never been a problem for him. He'd always had money and, when he didn't have enough or thought he didn't, he'd simply taken what he wanted. It had been a very good system his entire life. But that wasn't all it was. He knew as surely as he was standing there that it had never been enough. "Because I always wanted more than I needed and would kill anyone to get it. Even if I really didn't want it. And be damned the person who would dare tell me no." It was what made him the man he was, not listening to people when they told him it was impossible or couldn't be done. Or worse yet, shouldn't be done. "But that is neither here nor there. What's done is done, I always say."

The entire driveway to his house was overrun with cruisers and vans. Most of the vans were television crews, but there were also county vans...three coroner vans as well as a large station wagon-like vehicle. He wanted to see if he could sneak in, but there was no way he was going to get past this shit. The television program he'd been watching had shown there were people there, but not to this extent. Jerry decided to try the back part of the house and made his way to the opposite side of the drive. Christ, it was like a zoo, and he hated it.

There were only three cars back there. After tramping through the knee-high grass and brambles, he stood watching as a large dozer moved lazily over the field. The cows mooed at them but didn't do anything to stop their progress, and Jerry decided that if he ever got out of this, he was going to have them ground up as burgers. They weren't even fit for steaks as far as he was concerned.

"Stupid animals." He pulled out his gun to shoot the one closest to him, but something must have startled them because they moved deeper into the field. Jerry wondered again why this was happening to him of all people. He was a thief sure, even a murderer, but he didn't kill anyone unless they needed it and if they pissed him off really bad. Jerry put his gun away and watched the progress of the slow work.

The dozer stopped after a few minutes, and several people moved to the hole they'd been working on. After a few seconds, three more people rushed to the same hole. Jerry figured they'd found the body of the last butler he'd had. The man had been a religious zealot and had left pamphlets all over his house. And no matter how many times he'd told him to stop, he continued until Jerry took matters into his own hands and killed him. See? He'd been warned, Jerry told himself. That in and of itself should count for something.

An hour and a half passed, and Jerry relieved himself twice as he watched. Where he needed to go was less than a hundred yards from where the people were now working, and he could wait them out. He only wished he'd have thought to bring a drink and some food with him.

As he settled down near one of the larger trees to pass the time more leisurely, he thought about his niece and her mom. Her name had been Diana English before she'd married his dumbass brother. And Diana had loved Lindale too much, he'd always thought, and had not cared for Jerry at all. He also knew that Lindale had killed his wife because Jerry had told him that he'd fucked her and that she had come on to him. In reality, he'd never touched her. But Lindale had heard that Jerry was seeing someone else—another man from somewhere else—and he needed to make Lindale see that he wasn't gay. Not his brother, Lindale had said over and over. He would not believe that his brother might be different. Like his own fucking daughter wasn't.

Judith had been strange from the very first, he'd always thought, and ugly too back then. He'd not seen her since she'd been born the week before, and that had been when they'd been there at the hospital...the day they'd finally pulled the plug on her mom. He'd gone to see if Lindale would join him in his adventures now that the ball and chain around his neck was gone, but he'd been holding this wrinkled thing in his arms.

"What the hell is that?"

Lindale had looked up at him. He could see that he was stoned out of his mind as well as scared shitless. Not that he blamed him much. Christ, he'd killed his wife and now this.

"Are you going to keep it?"

"Yeah, I think so." Lindale had looked over at the sheet-draped bed that his wife was under. "When the baby was born, they told me it was time. She didn't even open her eyes. I'm glad; do you know what sort of trouble I could have been in if she'd waked enough to tell them what I'd done?"

"I doubt very much that Diana ever knew you are the one that killed her." Jerry had looked at the baby and decided it was the ugliest thing he'd ever had the misfortune of looking at. "You should just drop it in the dumpster. No one would blame you. It's fucking ugly."

"I'm going to keep her. She will have the women falling all over me to fuck me. What do you think?" Jerry had never been one to keep his opinion to himself when someone was stupid enough to ask, but he had that time. There was no way a woman would want to come within two inches of this thing, much less fuck his brother.

"I was wondering if you had time for a job or two for me. I know you been here a lot, making sure that she didn't wake and spill the beans, but now that she's gone, maybe we can take up again." Lindale was shaking his head even before he finished. "You're telling me you're going to go straight? I won't believe it for a second."

"Hell no, I'm not giving up my jobs. I just want to give the appearance of being a sorrowful husband. I have to wait to collect on the insurance anyway. They said it would be about thirty days." Jerry nodded, knowing that there would be a nice payoff for Diana's death. "Come back in a month and we'll get some things settled. I'll be flush then."

By the time Jerry needed his brother again three years later, he'd let some dick invest all the money into some kind of scheme. Or so Jerry had thought. It turned out that not only had the guy been honest, but he'd been good, too. When Lindale had been killed, he'd been worth millions, and he'd given it all to his kid for some reason. And he still had the brat. That was when he found out the kid was a freak. She was turning the channels of the televisions by moving nothing but her finger. The remote had been in the kitchen.

A noise to his left had Jerry looking around and bringing him back to the wooded area around his house. He saw a man coming his way, but he didn't look like he was searching for him but for a place to piss. Jerry watched as he pulled out his dick and played with it a bit before pissing like a fucking race horse next to a tree. The man had no manners whatsoever. When he started to jerk himself off, Jerry watched him for a few seconds before he felt his own cock stir. It had been a very long time since he'd been fucked, and he wanted a man.

No one had ever guessed he was gay except for his brother. He thought that Judith had known, but who the hell cared what she thought of him so long as she gave him what he wanted? Jerry had never taken a lover that he didn't kill afterwards, and he always made sure that he made himself fuck a woman at least once in a while so there would never be any questions. But he'd been celibate for too long, and freed his cock while the man down from him pulled his pants down to his knees.

His cock was small in comparison to the man's. Hell, Jerry knew that he had a small dick, but he could use it like a pro, he'd always thought. Jerry had tried twice to have his penis enlarged but had never found anyone who would do it for him and would hide the paperwork. Who wanted the world to know that you had a pencil dick? He watched the man again, hoping to come when he did.

As the man moaned and groaned, Jerry imagined himself sucking him. Licking his lips, Jerry put his finger into his mouth and imagined it to be Mammoth Dick's cock. Mammoth Dick, a name that suited his lover more than any other name he could think of.

His balls were tight as he continued watching, and when the first shot of cum sprayed the tree in front of Mammoth Dick, Jerry nearly cried out too when he released in his hand. Christ, the man could come, and Jerry felt his cock fill again while the man continued to squirt himself over and over. When he leaned against the tree, holding his limp cock in his hands, Jerry wanted to go to him and lick him clean, and that caused him to come again. He'd not had this much fun in ages, and certainly not from a distance. Finally, when the man walked away, Jerry cleaned himself up with leaves and put himself back together. Closing his eyes, he smiled as he laid there, relaxed, and decided a short nap was in order.

~~~

"Do you know where?" Agon looked around the house that had been done up in so much glitz that his eyes hurt. He looked at Judith when she didn't answer him. "Judith, you said he was here. Do you know where?"

"Not really. I was…I'm more concerned with the vault in the basement. I have no idea why that keeps running like a loop in his mind, but it is. There must be something in there that he's willing to risk coming here for."

Agon nodded and looked at the men digging where she'd told them to.

"What do you suppose is there?"

Agon was still trying to figure out what a man who had had so much would want with more. The entire house was packed full of things that had more value than some of the biggest museums he'd been to. And there were even more collectables in the basement where they were now. He looked at the shelf that held artifacts from the thirteenth century and thought about that time of his life and shivered. This was beyond covetousness.

Benny came toward them, and he knew that there was more bad news. His face told Agon that he was going to have to hold on to his temper that was showing itself more as they waited here. When Benny said her name, Judith grabbed his hand like a lifeline and Agon pulled her into his arms again.

"There are some things I'd like to ask you. I'm not sure you would know, but I have to ask." She nodded, and Benny looked at Agon. "It's not pretty. We've found…there was another vault in his bedroom that we discovered quite by accident."

"He did it." When Agon looked at Judith when she didn't continue, she buried her face in his neck. "They found some pictures of children. And…souvenirs as well. Clothing and…and things from little boys. Jerry has been collecting things for years and years."

It took Agon a few seconds to get what she was saying. And when he did, he felt his belly lurch. A man who did this was beyond anything he'd ever encountered. When Benny continued explaining to Judith what they'd found and wondered if by any chance had she been a victim as well, Agon reached for Boss.

I cannot…I need You. I cannot think what to say to her in her need. Boss didn't say anything, and Agon felt his heart break, not for him but for Judith. *He has hurt so many, and there are so many that he…why would he be allowed to live with so many people aching from his ways?*

I'm so sorry, Agon. I know that you hurt for the children, but this will bring them peace. To know that he will be getting what he deserved. It wasn't enough, and Boss seemed to know it. *For now, Judith needs you more than you need answers. I'm sorry, My son, but this is something that had to be done.*

I do not understand. How can we allow this to happen? How can...he has murdered them, the children that may have gone on to bigger and brighter things. Boss agreed and told him again how sorry He was. *I don't want your sorrow. I want justice.*

Anger boiled from him, and he had to back away from Judith to get some control over it. When she looked at him, Agon knew that he'd hurt her, but he didn't know how to control his feelings.

"You won't hurt him." He nodded, and Judith shook her head. "No, you won't. Even if you were to go out and kill him with your bare hands, what justice do you think it will give to them? You think it will give you satisfaction to know that you've rid the world of this monster? It won't. Not anything will but his own demise, legally and publicly. And only by the courts' system will anyone get satisfaction from this."

"Did you know that he was doing this?" As soon as the words left his mouth, he knew that he'd made a mistake. "I am so sorry, love. I did not—"

"Get away from me." He reached for her again only to be shoved back. "You touch me again and...you think that had I known this was going on I wouldn't have done something? Anything to save these children? You ask if I knew...did I know what he was doing here, and then call me 'love' in the same breath? Fuck you. Fuck you to hell and back."

As she moved away from him, Riss stopped him from going after her. He tried to push him out of the way but only succeeded in making him laugh. Finally, giving up for now, he asked him what he was doing.

"She will need time to cool off, I think." Riss looked over his shoulder at Judith, then back at him before continuing. "What did you say to her that would have her so angry?"

"I asked her if she knew what her uncle was doing. And Boss is mad as well. He...I cannot understand why He'd let this happen and not stop it." Riss nodded but didn't say anything. "I have messed up horribly with her. She will never forgive me."

"I would think you deserve it if she does not." Agon felt his heart break a little more. "You have done her a grave injustice by thinking she would not do something about this. And Boss as well. I believe what you have done today is 'bat a thousand.' Would you care to try to beat your record?"

"I will need to make it up to her." Riss nodded but didn't move. "Have you hurt Kala in such a way?"

"No. And I do not plan to either. Not that you planned this, but you did hurt her all the same. I have heard that groveling works well. And diamonds and chocolate. I know not what they have in them that makes a woman swoon, but Kala has said that it is the way to a woman's heart." Agon decided to have a conversation with Kala, but Riss was shaking his head. "You tell Kala what you did and you will have two women that hate you. She is very protective of the young woman."

"But what am I do to?" He hurt. His heart did as well as his body for what he'd done to his one and only love. "I will buy the store out of each item if necessary, but I do not know how to give it to her, and grovel, too, if she has no wish to see me."

Riss told him he had no idea and then left him. A cheer went up around the hole they were digging, and he found he no longer cared what they found. Agon had to think of how to rectify what he'd done. He thought of Lily and asked her if he could see her. In a few minutes, he was with her at the compound.

"I have messed up badly. Not just with Boss, which is bad enough, but with Judith. I have done the unforgiveable." He told her what he'd said and what Riss had suggested. "What do I need to do? Please help me."

"I do not think chocolates will work with your Judith. She is more of a practical girl. I would say to get her some, but not a house full. Diamonds?" She smiled at him, and he thought he might be in more trouble. "Have you given her a ring yet? To tell her how much you love her?"

"I have not. Should I?" She put out her hand in answer and he looked at the large blue diamond on her finger. "I should find someone to help me with this. I have no idea what she would like. I should buy her a diamond mine and let her choose the cut and color she wants."

"You think like a man." He didn't understand her since he was indeed a man, but said nothing as she laughed. "You think that a few baubles will make things right, when they will only help but not mend her broken heart. What you need to do is think of something that would please her. Not something that would get you off the hook."

"Hook?" She nodded, and Agon shook his head. "I think it would be better had I been watching Riss's worms for all these years. Them I know how to please. A bit of compost and a little water and they are happy."

"What are Judith's compost and water?"

He started to tell her that Judith was not a worm, but he realized what she was asking him. "She makes the most amazing jams and jellies. It is her hope, I think, to have a shop of her own, selling her wears and gifts. Kala told me once that she'd talked to her and that was what made her gush." He thought about Judith and her needs harder. "She has no confidence in her abilities either. She believes them to be horrors placed upon her when she had no choice."

"Benny would love to keep her on full time. I think she enjoys working with him." Agon nodded. "And you are right about her cooking. I would buy nothing else if I could. But she said she has no room to make all that I use. Apple jam is next on her list. As are grapes and peaches."

"She needs her own gardens. Larger than a few rows along the building." He thought of the orchards that he'd seen as a protector and wondered how one would purchase a farm. Agon looked at Lily when she handed him a paper.

"This is on the market now and ready to be purchased for the man who would have the cash. I was bringing it to Judith to show her, but I think you might be better off with it now. What do you think? Is this her compost?" The article told of a large farm that was going to be sold as soon as possible. "It has a large home that has not been renovated in some time, several out buildings, as well as a production building. I have not seen it as yet, but there are over four thousand acres that come with it. The land is covered in trees, an orchard as a matter of fact. There are also grapes, as well as a few other gardens. I have heard that there is also an herb garden that needs to be repaired."

"It is perfect." He read the rest of the article and wondered how to do this. "I need someone who knows about such things. I would like to surprise her with it, but I know…Boss would know."

"But He is angry with you, you told me." Agon nodded but knew that He'd help. There was never anyone as forgiving as Him. "Are you going there now?"

"Yes." Nodding again, he looked at Lily. "I cannot thank you enough. You have helped me when I thought all was lost."

"You'll get this and when you do, I'd like to be there when you grovel to her. It's the next best thing to diamonds to some women."

Kissing her on the cheek, he went to see Boss. As much as he knew he'd be forgiven, he also knew that it would not be easy. He'd been horrid to the people he loved and Agon was going to grovel as much as it took.

"My Lord, I wish forgiveness and Your help." It wasn't the best way to say he was sorry, but he needed Judith to not be mad at him. "I should like for You to forgive me and to help me make it up to Judith as well. I need Your help now more than I ever have."

Chapter 9

Walking along the deer path, Judith let the tears fall. It had been a horrific morning and now Agon thought she'd leave small boys to be killed. As much as she wanted to go back and strangle him, she knew that deep down he didn't really believe it, but it didn't make it hurt any less.

"You should know that I have spoken to him." She looked at Boss when He spoke. The man could pop in and out of her life like a ghost. "I am sorry as well."

"Sorry for what?" He walked with her for a few more minutes when they came upon a large bulldozer working. "They're finding all the bodies now. I have only had to point out one or two, but they're getting them all now. It's really depressing to think that someone could be so evil and yet…and yet give the appearance that he is as sane as anyone. I wish I would have known sooner."

"You have done well and all that you could, my dear." She didn't think so but said nothing. "The young boys, I'm very sorry about them. I knew, of course, but as all things…. Agon is very upset with Me as well. He thinks I should have stepped in and stopped it. I told him that…. But he has come to Me on another matter, and we are now all right again. He is very passionate about his love for you."

"As I am him. But You can't do it all." He looked at her and smiled. "I talked with Kala. She said You are looking more and more exhausted all the time. How do You keep this all from falling down around Your ears?"

"It falls a great deal, I'm afraid." The dozer stopped moving, and several men made their way to the area. "They have found yet another. Some they will never find, sadly. And others still will never be known. I think that sadder than anything that has happened here."

"I want to walk the grounds when this is all over. Maybe I can find a few of them on my own. Benny said he'd help me." Boss nodded but as they watched, two bodies were brought out of the earth, not one. "I'm going to work with him more, too. The commissioner is retiring next term, and Benny said he's going to run. I think he's a great person for that position."

"He is." She started walking again when the bulldozer's engine roared to life and started to move the earth from the ground to an awaiting truck. "Will you forgive Agon? I have never seen him so distracted before."

"I have. I...he hurt me badly, too. I know that he is under some stress, but he should have a better care as to what he says. But as I have said, we've talked." Boss said nothing, and she was glad. She didn't want anyone defending Agon right now. She wanted to bask in her anger just a little longer.

"He asked me to marry him. He said that You were the one to make it right. I'm not sure what that means, but he seemed to be excited about it."

"I will make it official, but you are wed in My eyes. I have something for the two of you, and you will soon see a difference in yourself. You have markings now that you didn't have before." She had seen the small gold crest that morning and told him. "It will change the day I pronounce you man and wife. You'll be a part of my Mystic Protectors. Do you know what they are?"

"Kala and Riss are ones. They said they are trainers of the new protectors. I don't know what You think I can do to help, but I'll do what I can." He smiled at her. "You know, I don't care much for that look. It tells me I'm in for a long, bumpy ride and my ass is going to bruise until I learn to flow with it."

"You have an odd way of putting things, but you are correct. You will be better off just going with the flow. Sometimes it is for the best when you do. I will help you when you need it, but I do not see the necessity of it. You are going to be fine." He laughed a little. "I think you will be surprised at how much you can contribute. You are a very brilliant woman. Others, not just protectors or mystics, will come to you for advice."

"I don't know about all that. I do have a few things going on now. And Kala wants me to open a bigger shop. I don't know if I'd have the time for that." She stopped at the edge of the fence line and looked out over the fields. "This is such a waste. Who would have all this property and not make a thing of it? Morons I guess, or at least the one that owns this is."

"You will make it right." Before she could ask Him what He meant, He spoke again. "I must go. There is trouble brewing elsewhere, and I am needed."

Then He was gone.

As she stood there thinking about her woes, she also thought about Agon. He was such a mystery to her. Not just in what he was, but just him. His manners and speech were like something from a Dickens novel. He was polite to a point where she wanted to brain him. Who the hell opened doors for women anymore? And pulled out chairs for them? No one she'd ever dated or even observed before. She turned when she heard someone clear their throat.

"I'm still mad at you." Agon nodded. "I think you know what you said was hurtful and cruel. It doesn't mean that I'm going to be mad forever, but right now, I think I like it better than you. My anger I mean."

"It was cruel of me, and I'm sorry. I am sorrier than I can explain to you." He touched her arm and smiled at her. "I have purchased you something. Not because you are upset with me, but because I have found your purpose."

"My purpose? What do you—?" She was suddenly standing in a field of trees. Not just any trees but ones filled with fruit. She walked up to the apple tree next to her and pulled the small fruit from the tree. "They've been neglected. Who would do something like this to such a lovely source of food?"

"The previous owners have divorced. I am not sure…it matters little. They are no longer in need of this place, as it is a sore spot for them. I asked Lily what that meant, and she said they had memories here that hurt. I wish for you to make the trees and us new memories." She looked at him as he pulled her along another row of trees, this one filled with what looked like cherries. "These have already bloomed and will again next year. There are peaches, too, as well as pears and grapes. I have never…did you know that with the right soil one can grow worms? Worms? Who would have thought that one would need to harvest worms? The earth is filled with them, and people would pay to have them harvested. People are very strange to me."

"I would imagine that they would think you are as well. But they use them to aerate the ground." What he said occurred to her, and she frowned. "What do you mean, make new memories? What have you done?" She watched his face as he flushed, and she was almost afraid to have him answer her.

"There is a house, but it is in poor repair. A barn and several out buildings as well. The barn alone is much larger than the building you work in now. And I have some of the others, friends of ours, working to bring it to code for you." She looked at the barn that was at least a hundred yards from them and noticed there was a tractor being worked on, as well as several people milling about the opening to the barn. "You will be able to move in by the end of the week if you wish."

"You bought this farm?" He nodded and pointed to the house, but before he could continue, she cut him off. "You bought this farm and all the buildings since this morning? How? Why?"

"Because I love you. And some because I have hurt you. I wanted to...you are not a diamond-and-chocolate sort of woman, I think. You are more of a get-your-hands-dirty-and-work-the-soil kind of woman. Buying you diamonds, as I thought to do, would have made you smile, but this would make your heart fill. Do you like it?" He took her hand again and bent on one knee. "I do have you a diamond, too. One that says that...that I love you more than I have ever loved a person or anything before. I wish that you would become my wife. Will you...I have messed up, this I am aware of. And I will much more in our lifetimes together. You will wish to smash me over the head with a close object and I will deserve it, but I would love for you to be my wife while you do. Will you marry me, Judith Craft?"

Her heart filled just as he said it would, and she felt her eyes fill with tears. "You drive me nuts. I love you, but you drive me nuts."

"Is that a yes?" She nodded, and he pulled the ring out of his pocket and slipped it on her finger. There was only a band showing, but she could feel the stone against her palm. "I would like to tell you something about this stone before you see it. It was given to me by a great woman. You know of her, of course, but I was there when she was…captured. There was so much more about her than written in the history books. Joan was a wonderful, special woman, and it was an honor to have been her protector."

Before she could ask him which Joan he was referring to, he turned the ring around. And she literally could not breathe. It was the largest diamond she'd ever seen, and if that wasn't enough, there were several other stones, all brightly colored, surrounding it.

"I'll need an armed guard just to wear this." When he kissed her hand and stood up, she held her hand up to the sun. Sparkles of rainbows danced along the trees and sky until she was nearly blinded by them. Looking up at him, she smiled. "I love you very much."

"And I you. But Boss wants us." She nodded and felt the air rush around her. Before she could blink, they were in an office setting. "He said now."

Boss stood up and grinned at her. She smiled back but was a little nervous now that things were going to progress so quickly. When He came toward them, she wanted to back away but stood her ground. Boss kissed her cheek and took both their hands into His.

"From this day forward you will be as one. No man, human or otherwise, will ever be able to pull you apart. No person will come between you, nor will you ever part, either in death or life. I pronounce you a couple for all time through love, compassion, and understanding." He winked at Agon. "You will need to work on your end with that."

He put a ring on both their fingers, and she felt the change immediately. When dizziness made her sway, she was picked up and held in Agon's arms until she felt she could stand on her own. When he sat her down, she knew that Boss had changed her.

"I have changed Agon as well. You are now and forever a part of my Mystic Protectors." He kissed her cheek again, and she looked down at the band. "I have fashioned it myself. And it will never come from your fingers, nor will anyone be able to harm what is Mine. You will be protected, as you are a protector. Welcome."

Judith found that while she didn't feel any different mentally, she did feel it physically. And there was something more. She knew as surely as she was standing there that she could fly.

~~~

Jerry woke with a start. He was afraid to move. It wasn't just dark but pitch thick black out, and he couldn't see even his body. Moving ever so slightly, he felt the roughness of something at his cheek and realized he was in a yard. Then what had happened came tumbling back. He'd fallen asleep in the outdoors.

As he had no flashlight or anything to guide him out, he didn't stand up. It would be just his luck he'd fall into one of the holes the dozer had dug and break his fool neck. Instead, he pulled his cell phone out and tried to see what time it was. Nearly four in the morning. Then he realized how bright his phone was.

Standing up, he used it for a light to guide him and started toward one of the heavy pieces of equipment that had been working while he'd slept. Amazingly enough, they were nearly on top of him, and had they come just a few feet more, they would have discovered him snoozing in the grass like a homeless man. Snorting to himself, he moved away from the area and back the way he'd come.

Every few minutes, he had to turn his phone on. He looked at his battery. Stopping to think what to do about having only about thirteen percent left, he wondered if he should simply wait until sunlight by staying there, or go on until he had no battery left. A noise close behind him made him turn.

There was no mistaking this person was the man on the dozer. He was big and his body, naked from the waist up, shone in what little light there was coming from the light in his hand. Jerry wanted to speak but was afraid that somehow he'd disappear and he'd be standing there drooling for nothing.

"I was sleeping in my cab when I saw you." Jerry nodded. "You been out here all night? Or you lost?"

"I was…both I guess. I think I got turned around and was trying to find my way back to the road." Neither of them moved, and Jerry turned all the way around to face this Adonis. "You say you slept in your cab?"

"Yeah. I had a fight with my…friend and figured I'd stay here to let him cool off." Jerry licked his lips, thinking of how much he wanted to beg this man to take him. "You queer, too?"

"Yes." Even to him his voice sounded harsh, heavy, he supposed. And for the first time in his life, he had no idea what to say to someone. "You lonely?"

The man didn't answer but walked to him, taking his belt off. Jerry felt his cock thicken as he watched him unsnap his pants, too. By the time he was standing in front of him, Jerry had dropped to his knees and was ready. As soon as the man's cock was free, Jerry was fisting him.

"Suck me off." Jerry didn't need to be told twice but took his thick cock into his mouth. "That's it. Suck me. Just like you wanted to do yesterday when I saw you. I gave you a show and watched as you fucked your own cock, too. Did you like that, me coming all over the tree? I thought of you watching me when I did it."

Jerry reached down to free his own cock. He wrapped his hand around himself as he gave the man head. As thick as he was, he barely fit into his mouth, but Jerry was giving it his best. When he started to fuck his mouth hard, sliding down the back of his throat as he did it, Jerry felt his own climax racing forward. But at the last second, the man pulled back and Jerry wanted to cry.

"Take them off. I need to fuck you." Jerry nodded and stood up. He was pulling his pants down around his knees when he was shoved against a fallen tree and his ass was filled. Christ, he felt as if he were being ripped apart. Before he could tell him it was too much, the man started to move as he wrapped his hand around Jerry's cock.

Jerry's body was on fire. His cock filled again, and his balls tightened up to his body as the man behind him pounded him over and over. Jerry knew that this was dangerous. The man could have all kinds of diseases, but, fuck, this was the best he'd had in forever. When he shouted he was coming, Jerry pushed back against his body even as his own cock released. He felt filled, and knew that the man's cream was spilling from him as he continued to pound. Jerry cried out when the man sank his teeth into his shoulder and came again.

It was several minutes before he pulled from his ass. Jerry winced when he did, the pain incredible now that he'd had his fill. But before he could tell him how amazing he was, he turned Jerry around and hit him in the face with a powerful fist.

Jerry fell back, falling over his pants and all the shit laying around. When he came at him again, Jerry covered his face and dick as best he could until his hand on his balls was jerked away. The man took him into his mouth and swallowed him down, even as Jerry hardened again.

He'd been sucked off before, but this man had such a powerful way of it that Jerry felt as if he'd been hooked up to a vacuum. His balls filled again as he fucked the man's mouth, both wanting to come and not because that would be the end. As soon as the man rammed his fingers up his ass again, Jerry came, screaming, and felt his world pinpoint to darkness as the man rolled him over and slammed into his ass again. Jerry never felt him this time; he blacked out from the pain/pleasure of it. Christ, never had he been fucked unconscious before.

When he woke, it was bright in the woods. He was alone, thankfully, and his pants had been pulled up but not closed. He rolled to his back, feeling every muscle in his body protest. Jerry had just had the fucking of his life and had no idea who had done it. Not that he really cared one way or the other.

As he lay there, he could hear the dozer running and wondered, just for a moment, what the man would do if he wandered over to it and asked if he could suck him while he worked. Instead, he moved in the opposite direction and toward the house, picking up his shirt along the way. It had been a good lay and now that it was daylight, it was time to move on. Jerry found himself whistling for the first time in a very long time.

There were two cops in the yard and one cruiser still there when he rounded the side of his house. He wasn't worried about them really, but moved into the back of the house to enter through a hidey hole he'd had installed years ago, before he'd gone to prison.

Moving into the house, he stood stunned at the damage that had been done to his home. Files had been torn open and papers were all over the place in his office. The carpet had been cut to shreds, and the chair he'd killed Jane in was cut up as well. Blood samples, he supposed.

Pictures, huge works of art that he'd paid a good deal of money for, were stacked in a long row down the hall like they were ready to be moved. Each of them had been wrapped in a dark sheet and had numbers written on them.

They were going to steal his art, Jerry just knew it. This was almost too much. The destruction and the theft of his things had him wanting to go out into the yard again and kill both men there. But right now he didn't have time to worry about them taking something from him that were just things…things that he had no doubt he'd be able to procure again soon. Jerry wanted to get in and get out.

Going up to his bedroom, he stopped again. Here the damage was outrageous.

They'd found his stash, he noticed first. That devastated him more than anything. He'd been collecting those pictures all his life. Very few of them he'd taken himself, but had only bought them when one or more of them appealed to him. The boys were all dead and buried, and Jerry wondered if they might be found someday. He planned to be long gone before that happened. But they were his photographs nonetheless.

Going to his closet, he nearly wept. Here the animals had taken all his suits and clothing and torn them from hangers and tossed them into piles. Even his shoes had been tossed away, and the handcrafted shelving he'd had made for them all was hacked at by what he could only surmise was an ax.

He was standing next to his bathroom when he realized how long it had been since he'd had a proper cleaning. Jerry knew that he was being really vain, but the thought of his own shower spraying on him had him stripping off his clothing quickly and stepping into the mammoth opening. It was like heaven.

He scrubbed himself twice before he felt better. His ass was sore, of course, but he was cleaned of the cum there as well. Smiling, he fisted his cock long enough for him to come and give him a good laugh. Then he got out and dried off. He was stepping into a fresh pair of pants when something occurred to him.

"They'll know I was here." Laughing again, he pulled two of his shirts out of the mess and put one of them on. The other, along with a few pair of socks and underwear, he put into a small suitcase. He was putting some other things into it when he picked up his shaving cream and thought of Judith. Going to the bathroom again, he left her a nice message. Then he picked up his bag and made his way to the sublevels. Time to get what he'd come for. He just hoped that it was still there.

There was an enormous hole in the floor, and he could see that they'd found his safe. Jerry didn't know what to do for several minutes as he tried to think where he could get some more money. There had been over seventy million dollars in that safe, along with several million in loose gems and diamonds. The rest had been passports and other things he'd need to run. Now it was all gone. He was glad now he'd scooped up his collection of watches that they'd not found as yet when he'd been in his bedroom. That would bring him a few bucks.

But all and all, he was thinking of all the ways that Judith was going to repay him when he finally got her. And he would, too. It wasn't just a thought now. It was a fucking need. He didn't really blame her for what he'd done. No, Jerry knew that he was responsible for his own actions. What he did blame her for was them finding all his things and now for destroying them.

"Fucking bitch." He was thinking of the several thousand ways he was going to extract all he could from her as he stood there staring at the enormous hole. She'd been a thorn in his side for years, and now…well, now she'd pushed him too far. It was time to take her out. No more keeping her for her abilities, but he was simply going to kill her. A noise from above him told him it was past time to get the hell out, and he snuck back up the stairs and out his hole. Jerry was making his way to the pool house when he saw her.

Judith looked for all the world like a normal person…long hair that reminded him of her mother, and a body that most men, stupid men, would find mouthwatering. He could only see her for what she was…a monster with tits.

"And one that is well past due paying for her crimes and what she's done to me." He made a quick stop in the pool house and realized it was going to be as fruitless as the rest of the trip had been, because apparently she'd guided them to the safe out there as well.

Jerry moved from the house to the wooded area behind it, his anger so hot that he wanted to scream with it. He was trying to figure out what to do when he realized that he should have charged his phone. Looking at it now, there was less than five percent on it. Not even enough to call someone. He had to sit down and make a list of what needed to be done right now. He found a tree to hide behind, pulled out his little tablet that he'd found, and started to make notes on it.

"A bit of food would be nice." Another thing he should have gotten while in his own home. "A place to charge up my phone so I can make some calls. Selling the watches will give me more time." Jerry laughed at his own joke. "Time and watches. I'm so hysterical."

He'd always had a shitty memory and now that he'd been using this tablet thing for a few months, it had only gotten worse. Jerry was typing in some of the other things he'd need, and was trying to remember everything but hoping to at least get the most important done. When the battery on it died as well, Jerry started repeating the most important things he needed immediately to try and remember them.

"Food, phone, buyer. Food, phone, buyer. Food, phone, buyer." He was walking along the street when he added two more things to his list. "Food, phone, buyer, transportation, and gun. Food, phone, buyer, transportation, and gun."

He realized he was drawing attention to himself and stopped speaking aloud. Nearly exhausted from his morning already, he stopped in a coffee shop to get something to hold him over. As soon as he sat down, he read the little paper tent that was sitting on the table. Charging station, it said. Sitting down with a mug of what turned out to be hot sea dredgings, he sipped his coffee while he waited for his phone to charge enough to at least turn it on. And when the couple next to him left, he got up to get the paper they'd left behind to see if maybe he was no longer the headliner. No such luck.

Jerry nearly leapt to his feet when he saw his picture on the front page. Pulling it tighter to his body, he looked around the smallish restaurant to see if anyone had recognized him. But they were too buried in their cell phones and coffee to pay him any mind. The headline touted him as being a murderer.

It took him nearly an hour to read the article. It might have taken him less time had he not closed it up several times simply because he refused to read the dribble that they'd said about him. But each time it was as if he'd had some sort of freakish inability to not finish it and was more pissed off at Judith than before. After his phone signaled it was charged to fifty percent, he left the restaurant in order to find a more suitable place for him to call his broker. It was too dangerous now to be out where he could be seen.

"I have some things I'd like to hock." Johnny said nothing after he had identified himself. "Just some watches I'm tired of and a few coins."

"Can't." Jerry laughed and started to tell him what the watches were, but Johnny cut him off. "I'm not taking them. No matter if they're all dipped in gold. You're too hot for me, and the thought of having your shit in my store, frankly, gives me the willies."

"You're kidding me." Johnny assured him he was not. "I've been doing business with you for years, and now my stuff isn't good enough? What the hell? You'll take it or I'll never do business with you again."

"Yeah, that don't bother me so much since every newspaper in the world has your picture plastered all over the front pages. I figure you have a few hours to be a free man, and I don't want you in my shop when you're taken. Christ, man, have you seen what they're saying about you...?" Johnny stopped talking for a few seconds. Then he screamed at Jerry. "Are you calling me on a fucking cell? Are you fucking insane?"

"What else would I be calling you on? You have to know they're raiding my house."

The line went dead, and he tried to call him back, sure that Johnny had not hung up on him. After a few tries, he realized that not only had he hung up, he wasn't taking his calls either. Jerry had several thousand dollars' worth of watches and no way to get them sold.

He was fucked.

Chapter 10

"The watches were a good idea." Judith nodded at the officer, a younger man by the name of Tony Kohl. "He's been to three different places and none of them will help him. Where did you learn to put tracers in something like that?"

"I don't know. It just came to me that he'd need money. And since we don't know where he might take off to next, it seemed a good idea." She looked at the monitors and wondered aloud, "Is it possible to see some property? I don't want you to get into trouble or anything. But we just purchased some land and I would like to know...you know, how big it is. It's hard to imagine when someone tells you."

"Sure. I'm sure Lieutenant Anderson would do just about anything for you." She nodded and gave him the address of the land that Agon had bought. As Tony pulled it up, Judith looked around the room they were in.

It was a pretty nice, empty room, but she thought of all the things she could do to it. This was...Agon had told her that he'd purchased this as a shop for her as well. As an outlet for her. She was still trying to wrap her head around the fact that they were married and he was out buying things like he was planning to live around here. She had no idea what would happen to them now that they were these Mystics.

"Wow. You bought this?" She looked over his shoulder as he brought the house into focus, or at least the roof of the house. "Did you buy the entire property or just the house?"

"All of it." The house needed a new roof, she could see. One side of it was peeled away like someone had used a large vegetable peeler on it. There were also a few broken windows lower on the house, but she could see that there was cut glass on the upper floor. "Do you think you can show me the barn?"

The barn was suddenly there. And to say it was large would have been like calling Agon tall. The man was almost seven foot. And this barn...she leaned in closer when he rolled the view to the rest of the yard. There was a garage that looked like it had seen better days, as well as two buildings that looked very new. When he moved back more, she could see the outline of the trees as they stood like long rows of tiny men dressed in leaves. She looked up when the officer cleared his throat.

"You do know that it's like four thousand acres, right? And that...Christ, lady, you're going to need a lot of workers to bring this place up to code to live there." She nodded. "If the house was in as good a shape as the barn, I'd say you could move right in, but it's a mess."

"It just needs someone to love it again." She wondered if that would be enough, but didn't say anything. In fact, she was slightly overwhelmed again. "The previous owners were getting a divorce. Did you know them?"

"The Mandrels. Not a great couple of people. I think they inherited the house from his family, but they didn't want to do nothing with it and rarely lived there, I think. She was more into fashion, and he was...well he liked his things, too. But his were up his nose and not in the closet. The land right next to it, that's the property that your uncle owns. Did you know that?"

She hadn't. And now that she could see it from this view, she could see something standing in a field, and a pool house. After a few more moves, she could see the top of the house. She asked him when this picture was taken, and he smiled at her.

"Don't know. I would say early fall from the leaves on all of the trees. Sometimes if you know something was there, like a car or something he might have gotten rid of, but is in the picture, you can date them from there. But I'd say fall. Not too long ago either. Probably a year or two."

She had no idea even if her uncle owned a car, much less when or if he'd ever sold one. She looked over the images for a little while, then moved back to her farm. She was making notes about things she wanted to see in person when an alarm went off. She looked at the officer.

"He's stationary for more than an hour. I set it up to alert me so I'd know to check out if he left the watches somewhere or he might have sold them. Could be nothing but...would you mind if I moved you to this computer?" She told him she was finished, but he opened the laptop for her and brought up the same screen. She was trying her best to get back into what she'd been doing, but he was talking on the phone, and she moved to listen.

"It's a hotel on Ninth. I don't know the name, as it's not coming up right now. I'd say it's the one that caters to the unwashed." She wondered what he meant when he continued. "Yeah, that's the one. Dollar Hotel. They charge by the hour, I heard."

She understood. It was a cheap place that someone could use for a quick fuck. Moving her chair closer to the officer, she watched as he typed things into the search engine and wondered what he was doing. A ledger appeared, and there were several names on it.

"The owner is a snitch of mine. Keeps his records on the computer so we don't have to raid him to find out what sort of trash he's keeping in his rooms." She watched as he moved slowly down the list, and one name popped out at her and she had him stop. "You know this man?"

"Yeah...let me think." She was trying her best to remember where she'd heard the name when Boss spoke to her. Smiling, she told the officer. "He was a friend of my dad's, I think. And my uncle might have mentioned him as well. I think he's a fence."

"Yeah?" He pulled up another tab and logged into an official-looking site. In seconds, he was pulling up the picture. "This him?"

"Yes. His name wasn't Charlie Brown back then. He was Tippy Balance. I'm not sure that was his real name, but my dad called him that."

Her uncle had introduced them, she remembered now. Her dad had been gone for a few days, leaving her alone and caged up with a loaf of bread as her food. When he'd returned, he was coked up and had a shit-ton of jewelry and bottles of drugs, like the kind you'd get from a drug store.

The officer pulled out his phone and started talking to Benny on the other end. She wandered over to the window and looked out. She watched a couple walking down the street who seemed to be arguing about something, and a person trying to parallel park their car.

The people on the street were oblivious to what was going on in here, and she was sure that even had they known, most of them wouldn't care. Going down the stairs to the main level, she saw that they'd already started to work on the shop. Some of the workers were covering up some of the pieces they'd decided to keep, while others were pulling down some of the paneling. She moved to the wall closest to her when they took the sheet away.

"What are you going to do here?" One of the men came up behind her, and she glanced at him as she continued. "Can we save this?"

It was a mural of some sort. All she could see from what they'd uncovered was that it was "Flou" written in a nice script. Dan, the guy who was taking charge of the project for them, had two of the men come and take down the next panel. Behind it was the rest of the word, and a large bag of flour with a few sprays of wheat near it. And a price of a loaf of bread. It was a whopping nine cents.

"I'd say we'll work our butts off to keep this. Do you want to see what the rest of the wall says?" She nodded and smiled. "Me too. And I would say that this is from the 1920s or there about. I remember that time, when even this was more than anyone could afford. Buying homemade bread was considered an oddity when most people would make it themselves."

"You're a protector." He winked at her and walked away. She was never going to get used to people not just being older than her by centuries, but looking like they were years younger than her. She watched as the walls of panel came down and showed a bit of history that would have been lost if the building had come down like the city had wanted to do.

~~~

Agon didn't have a lot of knowhow when it came to setting up a shop. In fact, of all the people he had protected over the years, few of them had had anything to do with shops, and more with making money through working a nine-to-five job. They'd been in them, of course, but never ran one. But this one, the one that he and Judith were going to have, was looking really amazing.

"Dan said that we'd be able to cover these with a protective glass that would save them from people touching them." He nodded at Judith as she showed him the advertisement they'd unearthed. "I was thinking we'd put the counter close to it so we could have a nice backdrop for it. I mean, it's pretty amazing, don't you think?"

He heard the hesitation in her voice and looked at her. That was when it hit him...she was nervous. Agon didn't know it if was because of what she was showing him or her ideas. He pulled her into his arms as he looked at everything.

"You have a wonderfully creative mind. I love this. I have seen these being painted before. A man would come in to work all day on something like this, and all he would get for his troubles was a man standing over him debasing him for the work. He might have had a passing talent before the war ended, but needed to make a living because of something that might have happened to him during the wartime." She leaned back into his chest, and he kissed the top of her head. "You have news about your uncle?"

"They know that he was able to fence all but one of the watches. The one he has on him now is at a hotel not far from here. I'm not sure what they're waiting on, but they don't seem to be in any kind of hurry to go and get him." He knew what they were doing but waited to tell her. "He was in the house long enough to take a shower. They told me that he left me a message. But they won't tell me what it was."

"It said for you to fuck off." She turned in his arms and looked up at him. "You are afraid of him?"

"No. Should I be?" Agon shook his head. "I have to go to the police station tomorrow to file a report on the things that they found. Benny said that I'd be getting it all when Jerry was arrested. What does he mean?"

"The house is in the courts for the moment, but once he goes to prison, everything will be left to you. It is the way we have had it set up for you." She shook her head and started to pull away. "Listen to me for a moment. The house and all the grounds will come to you because you are his only living relative. He will, through lawyers that work for us, give it to you to care for. Then once he is found guilty of everything, you will own it all. I think—"

"I don't want it. None of it. It's all blood money." Agon had told Boss she would feel this way. "You tell whoever is doing this to stop right now. I don't want it."

"You could do so much with the money. Things he would never have done." She continued to shake her head. "There are others, small charities that could benefit from your generosity. I do not want to tell you what you should do, but I would like for you to think of what can happen. Things your uncle will not like."

"You mean donate it all." He nodded, then shook his head. "I don't understand. Are you telling me to donate it or not?"

"Most places that can use a home this size will not be able to afford the taxes or the upkeep. Like many charities, they run on tight budgets. If you were to donate the house to be used and not give it outright, you and I and a few of the other protectors could help with the money. Keeping the house and lands up while they used it for their own purposes." He watched her work through what he was telling her. "I know a few of the protectors that would run the house as well. Boss thinks it would make a nice place for people to stay who need help getting back on their feet. Kala and Lily work with a few people like this who need a helping hand."

"He'd hate it." Agon smiled at the humor in her voice. "I mean, he'd really hate it. It's not really nice to think like that, but it does sort of sweeten the pot. I think it's a great idea. But only if he's caught can this work. And so far, I'm not seeing much in the way of anyone working to get his ass in jail."

"It is difficult, with the way things are being found, that they can...I cannot remember what Benny called it, but they need to catch him at something before it will be a done deal." She nodded but frowned. "You understand me?"

"You mean they have to catch him in the act, so to speak? No one else has to die, do they?" He shook his head, and she nodded. "Then I have an idea."

He was almost afraid to ask her. But she seemed to be working in her mind again, and he let her. One thing he'd learned in all his years of watching people was that some thought out loud and others in their mind. Judith was a person who thought things out quietly.

"I can lure him out. And he can try to kill me." He started to tell her no, but she put up her hand. "He won't be able to, of course, because I'm like you. But he doesn't know that."

"He can still hurt you." She smiled at him, and he wanted to give her anything she wanted. "I do not like when you look at me like this. It makes me think I am going to give in and you will win. What have you in mind?"

"Well, I was thinking of a way for you and me to come to an agreement." She moved toward him like she was gliding across ice. "We could also break the place in and see how sturdy the tables are."

He looked at the table and wondered why they should care if the tables were strong enough to hold a cup of tea. Agon looked back at her when she moved one of the tables from the group. As soon as she sat on it and spread her legs, he felt his cock thicken. She called him to her with a curling of her finger.

"Come here and let me show you." Agon moved like a man who was on a long leash and she was pulling the rope to her. He was willing to go where she wanted so long as she looked at him the way she was now. The closer he got to her, the more thoughts of what she might have in mind entered his head. By the time she had him sitting in the chair, Agon reached down to adjust his hard cock.

"I should very much like to feast on you." She lay back on the table and put her feet on his legs. "You are very tempting. Shall I show you what I want to do?"

"Yes." Her hiss of approval had him pulling her toward the edge of the table. He'd noticed earlier that she'd donned a skirt, and when he lifted it up to see her thighs, Agon moaned at what she didn't have on beneath it. "I've been thinking of you all day. How much I wanted you to eat me. If you do a good job and make me come fast, I'll suck your cock until you come down my throat."

He didn't think he could answer her, so he didn't. His entire body was hard and when he opened her legs wider, he nearly wept. She was gloriously wet, and he wanted her. Leaning down to her womanhood, Agon licked her from gate to clit and then suckled the tiny nubbin into his mouth. She cried out, but he didn't stop. Tasting her this way was just what he wanted.

Drinking from her was amazing. She was so wet and dripping more of her creaminess than he could bring to his mouth. Sliding his fingers into her opening, he was rewarded with her legs tightening around his head as he used his tongue on her as well. He lifted her with his hand so that he could taste more of her, and she cried out again. He looked up at her over her body.

She lay there with her blouse open and her bra unlatched. She was fondling her breasts and squeezing them so erotically that he nearly forgot what he'd been doing. Agon decided that he needed to be inside of her, and he stood up. She looked at him as he freed his cock.

"Come here and let me taste you first." He wrapped his hand around his cock as he moved to where she laid her head. As soon as he was close, she wrapped her hand around him and pulled him to her mouth. Agon moaned and threw back his head as she suckled at him. Leaning over her, he slid his fingers into her womanhood as she took him deeper into her mouth.

"Fuck me." He nearly fell when she commanded him. He was as close to releasing as he'd ever been, and he had to think for several seconds what she was saying. "Agon, fuck me. Come in my pussy."

Moving back between her thighs, he slammed his cock deep into her. She screamed out his name as she released and he took her pert nipple into his mouth and nipped at her. She screamed again, this time wrapping her ankles around his hips as he pounded as hard as he could into her. When he felt his own release coming over him, he threw back his own head and came, holding onto her hips as he emptied himself deep within her.

Several minutes passed, and he lifted her up and sat her onto his lap. She giggled once, and he slapped her bottom gently, then massaged the area before she turned on his lap and looked at him. Her breasts were so close to his mouth that he could not stop himself from lifting one to his mouth and suckling the tip before taking it into his mouth.

"You're going to make me want you again if you keep that up." He had no problems with her wanting him and pulled her nakedness closer to his body. Her womanhood seemed to wrap around his cock, and he rolled her back and forth over him. "I want to ride you this way."

Before he could figure out what she meant, she stood up and asked him to hold his cock. As she slid over him, taking him into her again, he held her hips. She was settled over him in seconds.

"This is riding?" She nodded and rolled her hips forward. Agon held her still while he adjusted himself and her on the chair. "I'm enjoying this very much. When you move over me this way, I can taste your luscious breasts as you take your pleasure from me."

"You'll come, too, won't you?" She moaned again when he pulled her harder over him. "I'm going to come this way. I love the way you fill me like this, so deep and hard. I could come just from you sucking my nipples."

"They are very lovely. I love the way they tighten when I nibble at them." He showed her what he meant by chewing gently on the hard tips. "They are one of my favorite parts of you. Then there is your womanhood. It has a flavor unlike anything I have ever tasted, and the heat that comes from you makes me think of hot fires and silky sheets. I love the way you make those little noises when you are pleased with me as well."

"Pussy." He nodded. "Say it, Agon. Call it my pussy." He flushed and rolled her forward on him again. He'd never said the word before and was slightly embarrassed to say it now, even if it was only the two of them there.

When she continued to beg him to say it, he stood up and laid her over the table again as he moved slowly in and out of her. She pulled him down to her mouth and kissed him as he pulled her bottom up to him. Leaning down to her ear, he bit her tender lobe and whispered in her ear.

"I'm going to come into your pussy." She screamed out her release, his name a mantra spilling from her over and over until she was hoarse from it. Agon let himself go, filling her with his seed as he held her to him. Never, he knew now, never would he ever love as he did this woman, and he'd die for her if she were but to ask him.

When she lay limp beneath him, he pulled her up into his arms and to his body. Closing his eyes, he thought of their bedroom and moved them to it. Laying her down on the bed, Agon stood over her, watching her sleep for several minutes before he dressed and moved to the lower rooms. He needed to make their house safe for them and others that came to visit them. Shifting so that his wings spread behind him, Agon moved out of the house and over the yard and buildings she was frequently in.

His magic poured from him and surrounded the house, filled all the wood and tile, the brick and mortar until he was sure that no matter what, they'd be as safe here as they would be in his own room in the other realm. When he finished hours later, he entered the house and could feel the power of it. The house was temporary at most, but he knew that soon they'd have their own home and it would be permanent.

Moving to the stairs again, he stopped when he saw him. Going toward the man that stood there, Agon pulled Galin into his arms. He knew it had been a hard day for this man.

"He died not an hour ago." Agon led him to the couch and sat across from him. "I shall never understand this part of our jobs. To have someone so young...it is the hardest on me, this part."

"I know." He did, too. When one of their charges died, it was as if a piece of them died as well. "You will have him in your memories for all time. There will not be a day that goes by that you are not reminded of something that he did, or said."

"I will...I think he was the best I have had in a long while. His humor and his goodness were something that I both admired as well as enjoyed. But I have...I have been rotated into the new program after my down period. I fear...I do not want a wife, Agon. I know that you are happy, as is Riss. But I've no room in my heart for a woman. You will please talk to Boss for me. I do not think I have the temperament to be with a woman and have her love me. I have no sense when to behave. I would rather joke than be serious. I do not want to change to have someone love me. I like me."

"I understand." Agon wondered if this rotation was a way for the older protectors to slip away. Most of the men and women he knew were tired, more than he and Riss were. Surely Boss would not be trying to get rid of them now. He listened to Galin for another hour, then the two of them parted ways. In the morning, he promised to go and talk with Boss, but Agon had a feeling it was much too late for his friend. He wondered how many more of them were about to be moved in the direction of the Mystics. It hurt him more than he thought it should. But seeing Judith sleeping in the bed they shared, he also thought it was for the good. He was in love with her and knew that if Galin met his wife someday, he'd be just as happy.

Chapter 11

"Hello?" Jerry had been awaiting a call from his friend for the past two hours. He had no idea what the man thought "I'll call you right back" meant, but two hours was entirely too long as far as he was concerned. "Bill, you said right back. What the fuck? Did you forget about me?"

"This isn't Bill." His skin tightened on his body, and he wanted to snarl at the woman at the other end. He had no more expected Judith to call him than he did for someone to say this entire week had been a joke. "I understand you're looking for me."

"No, not looking. I've been wanting a great deal more out of you than a simple conversation. Are you working with the police? Are they tracking this call so that they can capture me? I got news for you, it won't—"

"You're at the coffee shop on the square. You've been there for over an hour waiting on someone, presumably Bill, to call you back. I don't need for them to help me find you. I always know where you are and what you're doing." Her laughter rang through his head like a drill at the dentist office. "Now, do you want to talk to me, or bitch about how easy you are for me to find?"

"You know what? I thought I hated you before this shit, but I loathe you right now. And would gladly murder you without a second's hesitation." She laughed again, and he felt his temper flare. "You fucking cunt. What the hell do you want?"

"Tisk, tisk, uncle dearest. What a way to talk to someone who holds your balls in their hand. Don't you want me to help you now? Before you couldn't get me to you fast enough, and now...well, now I get the feeling you don't want me around."

He had to hold his tongue. Not only did he need her to help him, but he might just get the satisfaction of putting a bullet into her head, too. When she laughed again, he knew that she was reading his mind.

"I need your help. And I'm not going to lie to you about not wanting you dead. But as you more than likely know, I'm getting desperate." She hummed. That could mean nothing or everything, but he didn't care so long as she was making an effort. "I'm glad you've come to see that as your only living relative, you should help me. It's the very least you can do for me since you've all but had them arrest me."

"Oh, there will be a price. If nothing else, I've learned from you and Daddy that everything has a price. But that is not going to help us with the situation you've got yourself into, is it? So here is what I want. I want your house and all the property around it." He sputtered at her, but she continued before he could make any comment. "You won't need it. You're planning to leave the country anyway, and this way I can have a nice little place to call my own. Well, not my own, but you get the picture."

"You think I'm going to simply sign over all I have because you say you're going to help me? What happens if I renege on the deal, come back in a few years, and demand you give it all back? What then?" She hummed again, and he found that to be one of the most irritating things he'd ever heard. "Answer me, damn it. What do you really think is going to happen?"

"You'll get caught, go to prison for a while. You'll make an advance to the wrong person and you'll be dead, after being fucked up pretty good by someone called Ken, and I won't have to worry at all about you or you getting out. Of course, the trial. We mustn't forget the trial. There, you will be paraded around like the murderer you are. People will burn effigies of you. Then after the headlines hit the paper about how you've been convicted, there will be partying in the streets and people will never name their kids Jerrod again."

Jerry was speechless. If any one part of what she was saying was true, and he had little doubt that she was lying to him, he would be better off putting a bullet in his head right now. Judith laughed, and this time he didn't find it so much irritating as he did frightening.

"I want you to help, and I'll sign everything I have over to you. When? When can you get me enough money to get out of the country?" He looked around the coffee shop knowing that most of the people in there were undercover cops just waiting for him to make a false move so they could fill him full of holes.

"You've always been so dramatic. You're as bad as an old woman. The only cop in the place is the one coming toward you now. And you've met him. But in the event that you don't remember, I'd like for you to meet Benny Anderson. And don't shoot him. He might just make you piss yourself." The man sat down at his table, and Jerry took his hand when it was offered. "Good boy. Now he has some papers you need to sign. Don't fuck around on this, Jerry. Sign them or he won't give you that fat envelope that he has there."

The envelope was indeed fat, and he nodded to him when he was handed a thick sheaf of papers and a pen. Jerry didn't even bother reading it over but simply put his name where the man told him. When he shoved it back into his pocket and shoved the envelope at him, Jerry nearly snatched it away. He was thumbing through the hundreds as Judith continued.

"You really are a piece of work, did you know that?" He barely heard her over counting the money. He had counted to seventy one-hundred-dollar bills when he felt his arms being jerked up from behind.

"Jerrod Craft, you are under arrest for the murder of Damon James, Chad White, Marian Libby, Jane Holloway, Jon—"

"Wait. This isn't right. I'm leaving the country. See? I have the money to do so now." He picked up the phone as it had dropped from his ear when he'd been jerked around. Judith was laughing, and he wanted to hunt her down and shove all the cash into her throat and piss on her. "What the hell are you doing? We had a deal. I sign my shit over to you and you pay me to leave."

"You signed a confession, you nimrod. What the hell did you think I was going to do, let you walk away from all this? Get real." Her laughter was cut off when the phone was jerked from him.

The cop, Benny, again was reading the names of people that he'd supposedly murdered. He had no idea if he had or not. But right now, he knew it mattered little if he'd murdered one or one thousand. He was so fucked. Tearing away from Benny, he reached for his gun, only to have his face slammed into the table. Jerry was still trying to bargain his way out of this mess as he was being shoved in the back of a cruiser.

"She had a deal with me." The driver didn't even bother looking at him. "Judith Craft, she and I had a deal for me to give her everything I had, and she'd give me money to get out of the country."

"Did she give you the money?" The man sitting next to him startled him enough that he moved from him. But Jerry nodded. "Then I guess she carried out her end of the bargain, huh?"

"I know you." The man nodded but didn't help him out. "You came to my house...no my work. You came to my office."

"I did. Very good. It's good to know that I've made an impression on you. I just wished it was more positive, but we cannot have everything, now can we?" He laughed. "Like you, for example. Did you know that the man you had sex with in the woods has AIDS? Yes. You should have taken your own advice and not had unprotected sex. I hate to tell you this, but you have contracted the disease now as well. Too bad really. I had hopes...well, we all did...that you'd rot in jail for a very long time. I would say that's not going to happen now, is it?"

Jerry felt his cock shrivel. Dead. He was as good as dead right now. And it would not be by lethal injection, which by comparison would be much faster. No, he was in for a long and very painful death. He started to ask the man if he would kill him now, but he...he had feathers.

"You're...you have...." The man laughed again and nodded. "No, I won't believe it. There are no such things as winged beings. You're a figment of my...go away. I don't want you here any longer."

The driver looked at him twice as he sat in the back seat. If this man was a figment of his imagination, then he'd reasoned that the driver couldn't see him either. When Jerry glanced over to his right again, the man was gone. But there on the seat was a single feather, a long snowy white feather. Jerry started laughing and was still laughing when they took him to a cell and tossed him inside. And while he sat there, just calming from his hysterics, another feather floated from the ceiling and landed near his foot. Jerry didn't stop laughing until someone told him he'd feel a pinch and everything went black.

~~~

Boss sat at the table and said nothing for several seconds. Neither Judith nor Agon seemed to mind as they both were in a state of...He'd call it overwhelmashion. Not a word really, but one He used when He had nothing else to call a total meltdown of too much, too soon.

"It won't stand up in court." Boss nodded. He and Michael had gone over what was going to happen when it came down to it. "I gave him money to sign his confession. He'll say I paid him to do it."

"They will. But it will matter little." Judith nodded. Boss felt His heart hurt for the young woman. So much had been done to her and for her that she was as close to breaking as He'd ever seen. Boss looked over at Agon. He knew that this man was a perfect foil for her.

"Will he be let out?" Boss took her hand and shook His head. "I'm afraid he'll be let go. If he does, then he'll murder again and again. It might not be me, but people will die."

"He will never leave the court system again." It was the truth, and all she needed to know at the moment. "Have you seen the farm house as yet?"

"Don't do that." He started to smile but held back. "Don't treat me like some fragile flower because you think I'm going to explode or something. I don't explode. Tell me what's going to happen. I don't mean sugarcoated either."

"Your uncle will be convicted on all charges because he will confess. Not the way you had him do it, but he will confess. Then, because of his unfortunate sexual partner, he will die in prison in a few months. As will three other men he has relations with."

"Because he's gay." Even though it wasn't a question, He nodded at her anyway. "And what happens with the property? I know we talked about using it as a halfway house or something, but I didn't have him sign anything over to me."

"You did what was necessary. As for the house and all his properties, they will come to you, as you are his only living relative. The people we have in place will make sure that things progress in a timely manner for you. And you will get everything that was his in due time." She got up to pace, and Boss looked at Agon. "The building downtown? You are pleased with the work?"

"We are. I never...did you know that the protectors are enjoying this more than I ever thought? I mean, they are working nearly non-stop taking down walls that are not useful, painting them when the repairs are made. Two have even asked if they may work the counters when their time for rest has come. I believe they are having a very good time." As Boss had thought they would. "I have talked with a few of the others, Galin in particular. He is worried You will be finding him a wife as well."

"I am." Agon smiled, and Boss laughed. "You will tell him so? Or will you leave him to fumble through this as you and Riss have?"

"Fumble and fall." Agon looked over at Judith as she paced. "I believe the reward is much sweeter when you must learn as you go. I know that I have never been happier."

Boss felt good. Better, actually, than He had in a very long time. When Judith sat back down, He knew that her mind had settled all that she was thinking about, and now she would have questions.

"Will the others, the other protectors, come to my shop to work or will they be there to rest?" Before He could answer her, she continued. "I don't have a lot of money to pay them with. I could use the help, I think. Kala has asked me to supply the house and grounds with soaps and herbs, as well as all the jellies and jams I can make."

"None of the people who would come to you will need your money. All of them are paid well, and most of them will not want your money even if they did. It is relaxing for them to do something that requires them to interact with others. As for the soaps and jellies? I think it would do you good there as well. You, too, will interact with others and mayhap become less cautious of people." She nodded, but He could see the skepticism on her face. "You will be fine, Judith. By the way, have you chosen a last name as yet?"

"Yes." Agon took Judith's hand into his as he answered. "Riss took the name Trainer, as he should. It took us a little while to find something that would suit us as well. Judith has thought of Guardian. For that is what we will be to the fruits we have taken into our care."

Boss liked it and made a mental note to add it to the list. After the couple left Him, He sat down at His desk and thought of the progress they were all making during this time of need. Two of His best men were now happy, and He had so many more He wanted to care for. He looked at the wall that had appeared when He'd requested it. The pictures there were vast, and most of the men and women nearing what they thought of as their end.

He'd seen a difference in the few that had gone to the other realm. Two He knew for sure were benefiting from their work more than He'd hoped for; Dan for one. The man was enjoying helping at the new building so much that Boss had asked him if he would mind staying for a few more months.

"It would be an honor." Boss nodded, and Dan smiled as he continued. "I know that you have a plan, but if you could...I am not going to tell you how to do your job concerning me. But if you could see your way to letting me go as a protector, I would be most grateful."

"You are tired." Dan nodded. "I have seen this on you. Much too much I'm afraid. You are a good man, my friend, and I shall miss you."

Dan had gone away with a lighter step and had been working harder since their conversation. He knew that he'd not share his news. Boss knew that if he did, others would wish the same thing, and for now at least, He had work for them. Dan would do Him more good work as an earthbound protector than he ever would now as one who would take assignments.

Then there was Galin. He was going to hate Him for a while. He was sure the man would not want anything to do with the female he had coming his way. Nor would the female. She was much more headstrong than even Kala and Judith together.

Yes, Galin was in for a treat. As were the other men on this first run of Mystics. But this was needed. More than for the entertainment value, because it was a bit of fun for Him to watch them try to stay one step ahead of the women. But He knew that in the end, each and every one of them were going to be happy, and that would make Him happy. Boss looked up when Michael stepped into the room.

"Should I ever come in here and find my picture on Your list of candidates to marry off, I shall quit You so fast that Your head will spin for a month." Boss laughed and leaned back in His chair. "I am serious."

"I have no intention to find you a wife, dear Michael. You are too stubborn to try to find one that would suit you, and I do believe you would murder Me should I try. Nay, there are no plans for you to marry. Should you ever want to, give Me enough time to find the right one. I am not sure she is there, but we will try." Michael glared but sat down. "You are here for the trial, no doubt."

"I am. I should like to be there. I know that things are set now, but I should like to be there. I have spoken to him twice more, this Jerrod person, and I should like to torment him just a little. He has hurt someone that is very dear to us all." Boss nodded. "Kala has expressed a desire as well. I have told her she would be safer at home. She is most unhappy with me."

"As she is me. I have explained to her that she cannot take in every stray that she finds. And I do not mean cats and dogs. The woman has nineteen people that she is caring for at the moment. And Lily is beside herself with worry as well. What shall we do with her?" Michael laughed. "'Tis not funny. She is with child."

"She is at that. But I think she needs to care for the others because she is with child. It gives her something to focus on besides the children. In a few weeks, she will need to tell Riss he will be a father of not one child as he thinks, but four. He has grown worrisome about her as well. He is terrified she will pop soon." Boss had seen him look at her with a frown.

"I would like to be there. It will be a great thing to see him crumble. The man has been working hard to assure her that he can make this work, and she is worried he will hurt himself. The two of them are more suited than I first thought. They worry too much."

"As does someone else I know." Boss decided to ignore him for the moment. "The trial is in a few days. I'm glad now that we have been able to move it forward. I know that people want to have justice, but this will settle things for our people as well. It has been hard on them."

"It has been. Judith will lose the most, but she will be fine. Agon will love her no matter what, and the orchards will help. Have they...what of the house there? Are we able to save it?"

Michael nodded. "Dan has worked wonders. Of course, the magic that they're using has helped a great deal. But I do believe that he has found what he wants to do." Boss told him of the conversation He and Dan had had. "I'm very glad to hear that. He will do well there. I do believe he would have quit us before much longer."

It was nearly dawn when they parted ways. Boss sat at His computer and wondered not for the first time if He was doing what was right. It was not anything He would share with a soul, but He often wondered. As He set to work, He smiled at the names on His list for today. It might prove to be entertaining anyway.

Chapter 12

Jerry knew his rights and lucky for him, so did his attorney. Pedro Phillips had come to see him four times in the past two weeks and each time, he'd had better news. And now today he was going to be a free man. Looking down at the bandage on the back of his hand, he shivered again.

They'd drawn blood that morning. He'd been told it was standard policy in situations like he'd been caught in last night, but now he was terrified. The sex he'd had in the woods had not compared to the little bit he'd enjoyed last evening and the day before, but he'd gotten relief. But to be caught literally with his pants down had been embarrassing to say the least.

Everyone stood up when the bailiff announced the trial would begin. He had one rule to follow, and he was going to stick to it. Shut the fuck up, his lawyer had said. He'd handle it all.

The judge was looking over the file that had been handed to him once Jerry's crimes had been listed. Jerry looked around and saw Judith with her husband. He'd heard yesterday from Pedro that she'd actually married, but he still had his doubts. But he could see the huge fucking diamond on her finger and thought about taking it from her cold dead hands when this was finished.

Yes, he thought to himself, he was going to still kill the bitch. She'd fucked him over enough, and he was going to get his revenge. Pedro had told him if all went well today, or tomorrow at the latest, he'd be a free man by the end of the week. Before the next Monday, Judith and her husband would be dead. It was all that kept him sane.

The first witness was called, and Jerry zoned out. He wasn't allowed to speak, so he didn't listen. That's what he paid Pedro for. But the thoughts of what he was going to do as soon as he was out played like a wonderful porn movie over and over in his mind. She was going to suffer before she took her last breath, and that gave him a woody faster than anything he'd done in a while.

He'd been planning. A few favors had been called in and a few more I.O.U.'s had been signed. Jerry was going to have a hard time meeting some of the things he'd promised people, but he didn't care so long as she was dead.

"Are you ready?" He looked at Pedro blankly, not having a clue what he meant. "You're up. Are you ready? You remember all you're supposed to say?"

"Yeah, just answer what they ask me and don't fucking lose my temper." Pedro watched him for several seconds. "I'm not going to lose it. I've been waiting for this for a long while."

"See that you remember that." Pedro stood up and helped him to rise as well. When Pedro told the judge his client was ready, Jerry was sworn in and helped to waddle across the floor. They'd let him dress in his suit, but he was still clamped in irons around his ankles and his wrists. Jerry sat down and was asked his full name.

"Jerrod James Craft." The judge nodded, and the first man stepped up to speak. Before he could say anything, Jerry held up his hand. He was going to say this and be done with it. "I want her out of my house."

"Your house?" He nodded at the judge. "I'm not sure you understand what's going on here, Mr. Craft. But you're on trial for multiple murders. How about we table the house for a later time?"

Jerry flushed and looked at his attorney. He was looking at him like he wanted to strangle him. He had been told and told to shut up, but he felt it was his right to show Judith and the others that he was in charge. Fuck the system.

"You talk about your house as if you expect to be set free. Is that how you feel? That you should be a free man?" The other man—he had no idea what his name was—smiled as he leaned back against the table Judith and her husband were sitting at. Jerry glanced at his attorney, who was still shaking his head. Jerry hadn't practiced on this question, so he wasn't sure how to answer it.

"I do feel as if I should be free. Being locked up, well, I've done that before, and I don't think it's right that I be tricked into being there again."

"You were tricked? How so?" This one he knew. The man pulled a notepad his way before he continued. "You signed a confession to the fact that you murdered a great many people. It says here that you've also admitted to being a drug lord, selling women for pleasure, as well as a long list of other crimes. Yet you feel you should be free."

"I was sitting alone in a restaurant when I received a phone call from my niece, Judith Craft. She said she'd give me my money if I were to sign the house over to her. I had no idea that I was signing those false documents."

"You didn't read them, I'm assuming?" Jerry shook his head, but before he could clarify anything, the lawyer continued. "Why is that? A man of your obvious business sense didn't read over something that was given to him by a niece that he had said repeatedly that he hates? I would think you'd be wanting to bring in a whole table of lawyers for that." The room laughed a little and had Jerry's temper flare up.

"Yeah, I hated her, but she owed me. I needed her, and she failed me at every turn." The lawyer asked him how she'd failed him. "She has these freak abilities and she wouldn't help me with a few things using them. What sort of child doesn't want to help someone that provided for them? She's ungrateful."

"And how did you provide for her?" He thumbed through the file again. "It says here you murdered her father, even served twelve years for the crime. And during that time, you never had a single visit from her, and we can't find a single check that you might have written for her care. How is it you were providing for her?"

He had no idea. The man was confusing him, and he looked at his lawyer. The man looked livid, and he made a gesture of washing his hands. Jerry knew what that meant. He'd fucked himself and Pedro was finished with him. Fuck it then. If he went down, so would Judith.

"I'm not sure you would realize, but she was abused as a kid. She paid me to take out her father." The room seemed to come alive all of the sudden. "Her daddy used to lock her in a dog cage at night so she would do his

184

bidding. I never told anyone before about this, but it was her that made me kill my own brother."

"And you did it." The lawyer nodded when Jerry did. "Is it true you and your brother were having a fight? And that it was over the fact that you wanted Mrs. Guardian for your own use? The reason I bring this up is because you have opened the door, so to speak. And for this reason alone, you've been trying to kidnap Mrs. Guardian for several years."

"Who the hell is Mrs. Guardian?" The judge slammed his gavel down hard twice. "I don't know who that is. We were talking about my niece and her evil ways, not this other person."

"It's your niece, Mr. Craft. Her husband is there, and his name is Agon Guardian." Judith waved at him and blew a kiss. Jerry dodged it like a fool, and that set the room to laughing at him again. He was going to fucking enjoy killing the bitch.

"I don't know what you're talking about. I'm her only living relative and she goes and tricks me into sh...stuff so I get into trouble. I told her I'd sign things over to her so she could make decisions on my behalf while I was away. I never knew what I was signing because I trusted her. I'll never do that again." Because there would be no one to trust, Jerry thought to himself as he continued. "She was supposed to watch my businesses and property for a limited time while I was vacationing. And she had to go and try to make it more permanent."

Jerry was back on familiar ground now and looked at Pedro. He still looked mad, but Jerry thought he was getting it fixed. When the attorney asked him to read something for him, Jerry took it without thinking. He was reading it when he realized what it was.

"Is this what I signed over?" The attorney nodded, and he looked at Pedro. "You said this wasn't going to be brought up. What the hell are you doing sitting there? Get up and fix this."

"Are you saying this isn't what you did to all these people? I'm sorry, but as you've admitted several times, you signed this. I just assumed you'd read it at some point." The lawyer took it back and sat down. "It's all here that you murdered these people. How about if we go over each one and you tell us what happened to them?"

"Do you have any idea how long ago I might have done some of those people? Christ, it was years and years...you can't expect me to remember every man I put a bullet in." No one said a word, and he looked around the room. "I suppose each and every one of you remember every little thing you did from the time you were a kid until now. Fuck, I had to keep a record where I kept them hidden so I'd not bury someone there twice."

He realized what he was saying the moment Pedro stood up. Mother fucking shit balls of fire. He'd just confessed. He started to stand himself, thinking...well, he had no idea what he was thinking when two guards, these armed, came toward him.

"I'm not going back to jail. I was tricked again. I didn't kill anyone." The lawyer held up a notebook that Jerry knew. "Where the hell did you get that? That's my property. You give me that right now."

"So, you admit this is yours?" Jerry nodded and put out his hand. This was simply too much. "And you wrote all the information within?"

"Of course I did. What kind of fool do you take me for anyway? I have to keep things straight. I had people owing me and when they didn't pay, I had to know where the other bodies were so I'd not dig up somebody else. It's only common sense." His lawyer started for the back of the room, and Jerry called for him. "Get your skinny ass back here. This is your job, and I want you to get me free of this shit. I got plans for my niece over there."

"And what are your plans, Mr. Craft?" It was a trick question and Jerry knew it. What the hell did they think he was going to do to her?

"I'm fucking going to kill her. Look at the mess she's got me in. It's the least she deserves. I'm not going to jail again. I was tricked." The guards came toward him again and he realized that's just where he was going. "I'm not going back. I'm telling you right fucking now, I'm not going back to prison. I've got shit to do. And people to kill."

He was being pulled away when he looked up at the man who had tormented him several times over the past two weeks. Feathers and other things were left in his cell until he had started lining them up in neat rows on the bed above him. When he stood up, Jerry watched as he spread his wings out and walked toward him. Jerry could not believe that this was really happening to him. As soon as the man touched him, Jerry started screaming. The horror, he knew, was just beginning.

By the time he was returned to his cell, Jerry had been sedated. It didn't help him that much. He had a front row ticket to every person he'd ever killed and how they had suffered at his hand by a running movie in his head. And when he begged for it to stop, the movie would slow enough that he could not just see what he'd done, but also hear each scream as it rang into his mind. Jerry just knew he was going to be seeing this for the rest of his life.

~~~

"You should see the building now. I swear to you, it is as if we have taken a step back in time and the entire place is from the nineteen-twenties." Agon looked over at Judith when she didn't comment. She'd been quiet since they'd left the courthouse.

"I have been there. I heard that you are ready to open in a few days." Agon looked at Lily when she spoke. Her short shake of her head had him thinking she wanted him to believe that Judith was all right, but he could feel that she was not. Standing up, he took her hand into his and pulled her up.

"I need a moment or two, please." He didn't care if they agreed with him or not. He needed to talk to Judith. As soon as they were in the yard beside the barn, he pulled her into his arms. "You will be fine, you know. I have you."

"I know. But he's...I guess he really was going to kill me when he thought he was going to be free." Agon didn't say anything, but held her. "I'd like to take a walk. Do you think anyone would mind?"

"It will not matter to them. I wish to show you something anyway." They moved along the house, and he could see the roofers tearing the old off as the new was being put on the other side. He had to laugh every time he saw the protectors with their wings wide, taking stacks of roofing material to the top of the house. He wondered if any of them had ever thought that they'd be doing something like this. Agon waved at Dan when he came into view, then moved them to the orchard.

"The trees are doing great." He nodded and reached up to take a lovely apple from the tree they were near. "I've been working on some jam recipes yesterday and last night. I think I might have it."

"I'm sure you do." She bit into the apple and moaned. He knew it was delicious and when she offered the fruit to him, he took a bite as well. "There are peaches coming on as well. As well as the grapes that we trimmed last week are coming along very nicely."

He steered her to the field he'd been working on by himself. He had wanted to surprise her, but he felt she needed to see this today. He only hoped he had it right.

As soon as she saw it, she stopped and looked at him. Agon wasn't sure he'd done it correctly until she squealed. Delighted that she was happy, he followed her as she practically danced to the herb garden. Agon was so relieved that he had to sit down.

"It's wonderful." He nodded and watched her as she walked along the stones he'd placed himself. "You did this? For me?"

"I did. I had an idea that with all the other things you are planning to make that you would also enjoy making your own sauces. I looked up all the herbs I could think you'd need and had to go to several places to get the ones that were not carried here or in this area. I had no idea that there were so many purposes for one herb." She laughed as she pinched a sprig of lemon verbena off the bush. He'd learned their names as well.

She moved toward him as she brought the herb to her nose. Agon loved the way she moved, and he leaned back on his elbows when she sat beside him. As she moved over his hips, he reached under her skirt and cupped her bottom.

"You are naked here again." She nodded and rolled her hips forward. "I think that taking you out here in the woods would feel very lovely."

"I've been told that outdoor sex is amazing." She pulled her blouse over her head and dropped it beside her. "I've also been warned about something else. I've been talking to Kala."

He was only about half listening to her as he cupped her breasts into his palms. Agon loved the weight and feel of them as he rolled her nipple with his thumb and finger. When she ran her fingers down his chest, he felt a cool breeze and realized that she had figured out how to make them naked. But when she touched him again, he nearly cried out.

"It's my feather. And yours, too. I took one this morning. It didn't hurt me, so taking one from you was no problem." She ran the two feathers down his chest again and over his nipple. Agon laid back and let her have her way with him.

"You can use mine, too." He took it but didn't touch her with it. He'd been talking to Riss and knew other uses for the feather than to simply touch. When she lay back on the grass, he leaned over her and ran the feather over her nipple and down to her navel.

"I have been thinking of the night I found you wanting. I've never been told about the vibrating phallus before." She nodded and he moved the feather again. "To see you like that again would be a great thing."

He had to take two breaths before he could continue. The feather was almost forgotten when he saw her open her legs for him. She was wanton, and he loved her for it. Moving to settle between her opened legs, Agon teased her flesh with the feather. Touching her pretty womanhood with it had her moaning.

"Tell me what you wish for me to do to you." She moaned again. "I will make love to you soon, but for now,

I would very much like to give you pleasure. A great deal of it."

"She told me that you could use it like a vibrator. Show me." He moved it gently over her opening, and she moaned again. "More, Agon. Please, I need more."

He enjoyed watching her as he played with her. She was soaking the ground beneath her bottom, and he wanted to drink from her. Leaning down so that he could taste her, he ran the feather over her opening again and nipped at her nubbin. Her screams had him pressing his tongue against her over and over, lapping up what he could as she came again and again. When he lifted his head, he looked at her.

"Take me." He shook his head. He wasn't finished with her as yet, and he opened her wider as he settled between her thighs again. Drinking rapaciously from her, he knew that she was peaking because of the constant stream of juices that flowed from her. When she jerked his head up, he smiled at the look on her face.

"You're killing me. No more." He laughed as he sat up on his knees and rolled her to her belly. "No more, Agon. I'm spent."

"Not yet. I should like to take you this way again and feel you tighten around me." He moved up behind her hips when she was on her knees. "I have such a lovely view of you now, it makes me hard just to think of you this way."

He slid his cock into her sheath slowly. Her body rippled around him several times as she adjusted to his size. Agon had to slow down or release this way deep inside of her, and he wanted her to release a few more times before he took his own pleasure. When he was seated as far as he could go, he moved in and out, as he did his fingers over her womanhood.

"I love you." She moaned, and he felt her tighten again. "Release for me love, release so that I may join you."

She screamed out her release again and again. Agon pounded into her hard as his own body prepared for his peak. When he felt it roll over him, Agon threw back his head and roared, his entire body bowing back as he filled her. When he could no longer move, he dropped over her and then to his back, bringing her with him. He held her for several minutes before she rolled over and lay over him like a blanket.

"I love you." He kissed her nose when she yawned. "I'm really sorry I've been so moody. But I just…Kala told me that we'd have no children, because of what you are. I never really thought of it before, but knowing that it won't happen makes me sad a little."

"There are many children that will need us if you are willing. I know that next month Lily and Benny will be adopting two little girls into their home. I have heard that they are planning to take on three more before the year's end. Is that something you'd like to do?" She didn't answer him, and he lifted her chin. He could see tears in her eyes, and he felt his heart twist. "I did not mean to make light of us not having a child of our own. I only meant that—"

"No, it's not that. I was thinking…I didn't know how to bring it up before. But I'd like to adopt some children. Not yet, I think. We've no real house, and the business is just not ready for me to take the time as yet. But we have all the time in the world." He nodded and pulled her closer to him. "I want to have lots of them. Well, not lots, but more than a couple. Okay?"

"We can adopt as many as you wish. We will live forever and never age. Raising children will be wonderful with you as their mother. You have so much to offer them. I hope that…it is my dream to have a game of baseball and football in the yard someday."

"You'd do that with a girl, too, right?" He nodded, not sure what she meant until she continued. "Our children, male or female, will know how to play all sports and be able to do whatever it is they want. Even if they want to be a quarterback for the pros. It won't matter what sex they are."

He had a feeling he was touching on something dangerous and said nothing. She laid there for several minutes before she spoke again. He smiled when she sat up.

"I want to go to the barn and start on some jams. I have an idea for one and I want to play." She helped him to stand. "And just so you know, Galin is hiding out at our house right now. He seems to have it in his head that he's going to be married soon. I had no idea that he was seeing someone."

"He believes that Boss has it in His head to marry all of us off once we are put into the rotation He has devised." Agon dressed as he continued. "I have spoken with Him and He has confirmed what Galin thinks, but I have said nothing to him. I think it would be more fun to watch him try to get away. Much like I did at first."

"I didn't want you either. I'm sure once she is known to us, things will go much better for him and her." For some reason, Agon thought that was not going to be the case. Galin did not want a wife at all. "And no matter what he thinks, I'm pretty sure that it's going to happen."

"I believe so as well."

They made their way to the barn, and he told her he'd see her inside. He'd seen someone in the distance that he never wanted to talk to, and he waited for her to close the door before he moved toward him. Agon stopped when he was still a few feet away.

"Is this a way to treat an old friend? Come to see me, Agon, and we will talk." Agon didn't move, and the man laughed. "I see. You're being very cautious."

"What do you want, Markum? I've no use for you. And we were not friends. You were told to stay away from us." He looked back at the barn hoping that Judith would stay there. "Say what you wish, then leave."

"I came to see if you have changed your mind. It has been a long time, and things have changed a little since we last were together." When Markum took a step toward him, Agon took two back. "You do not wish to embrace an old friend?"

"As I have said, we were not friends at all." He reached for Michael and told him to come to him. "You would do well to leave here now. There are a great many protectors here, and they will not be happy to find you among us."

"You will not tell on me. I have something you want." Agon didn't move but felt Michael appear beside him. "Ah, the great Michael has come to rescue his little sheep. Very unfair of you, Agon, to call him to us. Especially when I have gone to so much trouble to hide myself from him."

"You are to leave here now, Markum. You are not welcome in this area." Markum didn't move, not even when Michael drew his swords. "The boundaries are keeping you from entering this area. But I may pass them. Come here again and I will show you the wrath of my weapons."

"I'm no longer the protector that you tossed from the realm. I've grown stronger as the world gets meaner. I thrive where I could not before. I am strong because of the evil in this world. You will find that if you try to conquer me now, I will not fall so easily."

Agon pulled his own sword from the air as he felt the other protectors in the area come to his aid. Thankful for the help, he still worried for Judith. When she spoke behind him, he didn't turn but stilled as she spoke.

"I know who you are." Markum laughed. "You're that asshole that I had some dealings with a few years back. I thought I told you to stay the hell away from me."

"You smell of sex. Have you been playing the field again?" Agon heard her sharp intake of breath and nearly reached for her. "Have you found a new job, Judith dear, of fucking the protectors? I assure you that you could do much better. Come to me…or better yet, invite me to come to you."

He was commanding her, and Agon had a sudden fear for his wife. But when she laughed, he turned to stare at her as she confronted Markum.

"Does that usually get you laid? I'm betting you use your hand more often than not. Are you sore stroking your cock and your own ego?" Michael snorted, and Agon had a feeling he was choking on his own laughter. "Oh wait, I know why you're so bent out of shape. You think we should all bow down before you and kiss your ring or some shit. Well I got news for you, tiny dick, I bow before no demi-god, especially one like you."

"You will heed what you say, Judith. There is more power in my body than there was when first we met." She lifted her hand to him and made a mocking sign at him. Agon felt as if he were watching a game and the combatants were picking their weapons.

"And you talk too fucking much. I'm sure you think you're all that, but I have news for you." She looked to her left, and Agon saw Lily and Kala standing there. They looked as formidable as he'd ever seen them. "The three of us can still kick your ass and then wipe up the floor with you. So I want you to crawl back into that hole you've managed to slither out of and fuck the hell off. Be gone."

Markum disappeared, and they all stood still as they turned to Judith. To say he was impressed would have been a gross understatement of his feelings right now. Michael sheathed his sword first, then the others followed.

"He will return." Judith nodded at Michael when he spoke. "And when he returns, he will not be happy with you. How did you know to send him away that way?"

"I guessed, I guess you could say. I know that sounds really stupid, but when a little dog, that would be him in this case, thinks he can come into my little piece of heaven and start throwing shit around, a bigger dog, or bitch in this case, has to show him who is boss. Well, bosses. I needed the rest of the females here to back me up."

"You guessed about banishing a demi-god? Where do you...what if you were wrong? He may have harmed you, then what?' She grinned at Michael, and he flushed. "Next time you have such a guess, I would please have you clear it through me first. I do know a thing or two as well."

"Yeppers, I most certainly will. I should have come to you first, but...well, but there you have it. Fight bitch with bitch, I suppose." She took Agon's hand. "Markum, that wasn't his name when I knew him. But he doesn't know we're married, does he?"

"I do not believe so. Would it matter if he did?" She nodded, and he kissed her hand as the others dispersed back to their jobs. "Why would a thing like this matter to him?"

"He'd use it against us, I think. I don't think he plays well with others." Agon laughed, and she smiled at him. "He didn't hurt you, did he? I called to the others when I felt you were in trouble. I didn't know what to do, but Lily said she'd come. Kala was with her."

"He was more afraid of the three of you than he was of Michael. Why do you suppose that is?" She shrugged, and he watched her face. "You will not tell me? I am your husband. You should not keep things from me."

"I really don't know. But I will keep an eye out for him from now on." They moved back to the barn, and she spoke of the apples she'd had brought to her. Agon was fearful for them all if Markum should return. He decided that he'd keep an eye out as well.

Chapter 13

Dusty McGee watched the second hand moved around the clock face. It would only need to pass the twelve eighteen more times before she could go in and see her sister again. If Rose lived that long. It had been a long and hard week, and she had a feeling it wasn't going to get much better. She looked over at Kip, her sister's son. He was watching the clock, too.

"You can go first." He glared at her, and she took a deep breath. "They will only let us stay there for ten minutes, and I thought you'd want to go in first this time. She might be—"

"I don't care if I ever see her again. What the hell was she thinking, anyway?" Dusty didn't answer him because, frankly, she had no idea what her sister had been thinking. Not in the way she'd been hurt, nor what the lawyer had told Dusty that morning. But Kip didn't know that part yet.

"You don't mean that. Not seeing your mom again will hurt you someday." He got up, and she was again surprised at how tall he'd gotten. "Kip, she's your mom, no matter what she'd been doing."

"Fuck off." His favorite thing to say to her since she'd gotten here last week. And when he walked away from her, she didn't go after him this time. To be honest, he was wearing her out more than visiting her dying sister was.

Eight days ago, she'd been on her way to work when she'd gotten a phone call. A very nice officer had told her that her sister had been in an accident and that she was asking for her. This had happened before with Rose. She'd get in a jam, hurt herself, and call for her to bail her out. Dusty was ready to tell the officer she didn't have time when he cleared his throat. In that second, she knew that this time was different.

"She's not going to live long, Miss McGee. The car that she hit knocked her into a busy intersection and she was hit three more times before she was thrown from the car. Her injuries are...they're horrific, and her body is broken."

"Where is Kip? Her son? Was he with her?" He didn't say anything for several seconds, and she knew he was thinking of a way to tell her he'd not made it. "Please tell me he went quickly."

"We weren't aware there was a boy. I'm sending someone to her house now. Do you know anything that would help us talk to him?" Did she? Not really. She barely knew the boy herself since she and Rose had parted company about eight years ago.

"He's twelve now...no wait, not yet. He's eleven. But he has a mouth on him like an adult and will cut you to ribbons without a single thought." She closed her mouth when she realized what she'd just said. "I'm sorry. I'm...I'm on my way. I'll be there in the...where will I be coming to?"

"Mercy General. She's in surgery now, but I had to assure her I'd call you before she'd let them take her in." Sounded like Rose, stubborn to a fault. "Do you need someone to pick you up?"

"Actually, I need more than that. I don't know where my sister has been for the past eight years. We never were very close." She pulled off the highway and sat there wiping at the tears. "Is she really dying? I mean, she's pulled crap like this before. Having someone call me to tell me she was grave only to find her healthy as an ox when I got there. Tell me this is like that. I won't be mad. I swear I won't. I'll just give her whatever it is she wants and leave again."

"I'm sorry, Miss McGee. This is the real deal." He told her what city and state her sister was in and asked her if she wanted him to pick her up at the airport. She told him no, that she'd rent a car. After she hung up, Dusty called her assistant.

"I'm going away for a few days. There's some family problems I have to take care of." Denise Bush laughed. "I'm serious. My sister has had an accident."

"How bad? And don't worry about a thing. I'll take care of it. Will you need for me to set some things up for you? Hotel, car rental while there?" Dusty loved this woman because of all she was. "I'm calling in a few favors now to get you whatever you need. Wait, it might help if I knew where you needed this done."

After she explained where she was going, she hung up. It wasn't until she was at the airport that she realized she might not make it in time to see her. That had been so long ago that Dusty wasn't sure she'd ever feel as if she wasn't in a dream. A nightmare, she supposed.

"Miss McGee?" She looked up at the man who was smiling down at her. "It's time for you to see her again. I've looked for Kip, but he said that he...he is coming now."

Dusty followed the man, a male nurse, down the hall again. She had no idea why it was so far away from the intensive care unit, but it seemed miles since she'd gotten up. When they were outside the door, he turned to look at her.

"She will not be with us much longer. If you can, I would suggest you say your goodbyes now." She nodded and looked down the hall as Kip came toward her. "I will allow you both in together this time. Please...you can stay as long as you wish."

Kip took her hand, and she squeezed it tightly. As they entered the room, the machines keeping her sister alive were eerily quiet. She looked at the form on the bed, having just yesterday stopped thinking of the broken body as her sister any longer. When the officer had told her she was bad, he'd not even been close to what had happened to her.

"Mom?" Kip moved to the bed and held his mother's hand. She stayed back, giving him all the time he needed. She tried to think of the last time she'd spoken to her sister, and all she could remember, like every other time, was that they'd fought. As they did all the time. When Kip looked at her, she realized that he had said something.

"She's going to die." Dusty nodded and moved toward him. "What the heck am I going to do now? I have nothing. They won't let me...I called a lawyer, and he said that I wouldn't be able to stay in my house any longer, that I wasn't old enough."

"You're coming with me. She, your mom, made arrangements for me to take care of you if anything should—"

"I'm not going with you. I don't even like you. And neither did my mom. Why the heck would she say something like that? You're a liar. I'm not going anywhere with you. Mom will get better, you'll see."

Her heart, already so tender she wasn't sure if it was beating or not, shattered. He started sobbing, and she wanted to go to him and even took a step toward him when the machine near Rose's head started screaming at them. She was shoved out of the way as two nurses came into the room, but neither of them made a move toward her sister. It had been predetermined that Rose was too far gone for them to try to resuscitate.

Dusty stepped into the hall when the doctor pronounced her deceased. She could hear Kip in the room screaming at them to wake her up, but Dusty had to get away. She was moving to the front doors when a man stepped in front of her.

"You will survive this." She shook her head and tried to step around him, but he moved with her. "Look at me, Dusty. You will survive this. And you will be stronger for it."

"Stronger? I've never been strong in my life. My sister is dead, and her son hates me. And as of twenty seconds ago, he's my responsibility. I don't know what to do with a kid. I can't even keep myself straight without an assistant." She realized she was screaming at him and took a deep breath. "I'm going home now. If he doesn't want me, I guess there isn't a damn thing I can do to make him."

"Simply love him."

She looked up when she realized she was sobbing again and the man was gone. She stood there for several minutes before she moved out of the building and into the fresh air.

She had to get arrangements made. Call people and make sure her nephew was going to be well. Dusty wasn't sure what happened now, but she didn't want him any more than he did her. Sitting there for a few more minutes, Dusty knew two things. She was more alone than she'd ever been, and as of right now, she was as depressed as she ever would be again. Standing, she entered the hospital. The sooner she was finished with this, the quicker she could get moving again.

About the Author

Kathi Barton, author of the bestselling series Force of Nature, lives in Nashport, Ohio with her husband Paul. In addition to writing full time Kathi likes to spend time with her eight grandkids, three children and three children-in-laws. She writes to relax and have fun.

Her muse, a cross between Jimmy Stewart and Hugh Jackman brings them to life for her readers in a way that has them coming back time and again for more. Her favorite genre is paranormal romance with a great deal of spice. You can visit Kathi on line and drop her an email if you'd like. She loves hearing from her fans. aaronskiss@gmail.com.

Follow Kathi on her blog:
http://kathisbartonauthor.blogspot.com/

www.ingramcontent.com/pod-product-compliance
Lightning Source LLC
Chambersburg PA
CBHW032128170626
46808CB00006B/2147